The Case of the
Ice-Cold Hands

Erle Stanley Gardner

BALLANTINE BOOKS ● NEW YORK

ISBN 0-345-35939-9

This edition published by arrangement with William Morrow and Company, Inc.

Manufactured in the United States of America

First Ballantine Books Edition: February 1989

Foreword

My good friend, Dick Ford (Richard Ford, M.D., Massachusetts State Police Pathologist, Senior Medical Examiner of Suffolk County, Boston, Head of the Department of Legal Medicine at Harvard Medical School, and to whom I have already dedicated a Perry Mason book), has pointed out from time to time the necessity for closer liaison between law enforcement, forensic pathology and legal medicine.

Heaven knows how many murders Dr. Ford has investigated. No one knows how many times he has been able to give to the police a clue to a crime, suggest a suspect, or point out a line of thought resulting in the solution of the case. And in several instances that I know of, his shrewd counsel has resulted in sparing an innocent man from being charged with a murder which turned out to be no murder at all, but an accidental death or a suicide.

For some sixteen years now, Dr. Ford has been working with Joseph B. Fallon of the Boston Police Department. Fallon has recently, by his own decision, retired with the rank of Deputy Superintendent at the age of sixty-three.

From time to time over the past years, Dr. Ford has told me about Fallon, about his skill in interrogation, about his insistence that a man must in fact be held innocent until the evidence conclusively proves his guilt.

Dr. Ford insists that Fallon is one of the shrewdest interrogators he has ever encountered: a man who doesn't resort to browbeating, who remains a gentleman at all times, who is patient and considerate, careful but tenacious.

Fallon has the rare gift of being able to teach and at the same time to put his theories into execution. He leaves behind him in the Boston Police Department well-trained investigators, hand-picked by himself, of whom he can be proud. He has taught them and he has taught them well. Despite his retirement, his influence will continue to be felt in the department through the activities of these well-trained investigators.

The point I wish to make is that legal medicine is of great value to the public, that its value can be enhanced by police officers who have the ability and the mentality to work hand in hand with the brightest brains in the field of legal medicine—men who are big enough to share the credit where there is credit, and who are strong enough to stand up and say that the police haven't a case when circumstances are such that the police do *not* have a case.

For some years now I have had firsthand information concerning many of Joe Fallon's cases, the manner in which he works, his thoroughness, his courtesy, his uncanny ability as an interrogator and his unswerving integrity to his uniform and to his ideals.

It is for these admirable qualities that, on his retirement, I dedicate this book to an outstanding officer,

JOSEPH B. FALLON, Deputy Superintendent
    of the Boston Police Department.

                    Erle Stanley Gardner

Cast of Characters

Chapter 1

Della Street, Perry Mason's confidential secretary, said, "This is a brand-new one, Chief."

Mason looked up from the book he was studying, shook his head and said, "There aren't any really *new* ones, Della."

"This one is," Della Street said. "You have a client waiting in the outer office who says she can give you twenty minutes and no more."

"*She* can give *me* twenty minutes?" Mason asked.

"That's right."

"Well, that *is* a new wrinkle," Mason admitted. "What's her name, Della?"

"Audrey Bicknell."

"Age?"

"Late twenties."

"Blonde, brunette, redhead?"

"Very much the brunette," Della said. "Very fiery, very strong personality—something of a black opal. You'll like her."

"Honest?" Mason asked.

"I'd say she was on the up and up, but she's laboring under a terrific strain. She looked at her wristwatch five times in the two or three minutes I was talking with her, finding out her name and address. She's a secretary who is at present out of work, unmarried, living in an apartment which she kept up by herself but is now looking for some other young woman similarly employed to share expenses."

"Did you ask her what she wanted to see me about?"

"Yes. She said she had time to explain it only once and that she'd prefer to go over it with you. She said it was a matter of some importance."

"All right," Mason said, "let's get her in, Della, and see what it's all about. I take it she's good-looking."

Della Street slowly moved her hands in a line signifying curves and contours.

Mason grinned. "What are we waiting for, Della? What's holding us back?"

"Just feminine intuition," Della Street said, "the expression on her face when she said she couldn't tell me what she wanted to see you about. I have an idea that this girl is accustomed to putting things across with the aid of her dynamic, colorful personality, and she felt this particular approach would be more effective with a man than with a woman."

"All right, we'll see her," Mason said. "You have now aroused my curiosity to such a point that I'd never let her leave the office, even if she does come in conflict with our four o'clock appointment."

"You have ten minutes," Della Street said.

"And *she's* willing to give *me* twenty," Mason observed.

"About seventeen now," Della Street said, looking at her wristwatch, and then retreating to the outer office to return shortly with Audrey Bicknell in tow.

"Miss Bicknell, Mr. Mason," she said.

Audrey Bicknell came forward with a quick, impulsive motion, giving Mason her hand and smiling up at him with dark, intense eyes.

"*So* nice of you to see me, Mr. Mason. I know that it ordinarily takes an appointment, but this is a matter of the greatest urgency, and I . . ." She broke off to look at her wristwatch, then smiled, said, ". . . have to cut this exceedingly fine. Would you mind if I just began talking and . . . well, sort of skipped all the preliminaries?"

"Go ahead," Mason said.

"I've given your secretary my name and address," she

2

said. "I can tell you very quickly what I want. I take it you've been to the races?"

"I've been to the races."

"And are familiar with the procedure of betting at the track?"

Mason nodded.

"I have here five one-hundred-dollar tickets on horse number four, whose name is Dough Boy and who is in the third race this afternoon," she said. "At the time the tickets were purchased the estimated odds were nearly fifty to one. I suppose that a bet of this size will pull the odds down somewhat, and of course I know the estimated odds aren't controlling, but— Well, the horse will pay off big."

"If he wins," Mason said. "Or perhaps I should say if he has won, since the race is undoubtedly over by this time."

"If he has won," she repeated.

"And what do you want me to do?" Mason asked.

"I want you to take these tickets and hold them. If the horse has won, I want you to cash the tickets and deliver the cash to me in accordance with instructions."

"Now, just a minute," Mason said. "You purchased these tickets yourself?"

"Yes."

"May I ask if you play the races regularly, if this is something you do— "

"This is the third time in my life that I ever made a bet—that is, in this manner. I have sometimes placed two-dollar bets through . . ." Her eyes lowered. "Through bookies."

"How did you find the bookies?" Mason asked.

"There was a young man in the office where I worked who knew where to place bets, and sometimes we'd go in on a pool, or sometimes . . . well, sometimes I'd bet."

"Never more than two dollars?"

"No."

"You must have had some pretty hot information on this horse," Mason said.

"Does that make any difference?"

"It doesn't make any difference in the cashing of the tickets," Mason said, "but I'm trying to get the complete picture so I can protect you and so I can . . . well, frankly, so I can protect myself."

"There's no protection needed as far as *you* are concerned," she said. "All *you* have to do is go to the window tomorrow afternoon—the window that is reserved for bets on winning horses that came in the day before— present your tickets, get the money and then wait for my instructions."

"And if the horse has lost?" Mason asked.

"Then you won't have to go to the race track," she said, smiling.

"You seem fairly confident the horse is going to win or has won."

"I certainly wouldn't bet on a horse I thought was going to lose," she said. "But you're wrong if you feel I have any advance information. I pick my horses by hunches, intuitively, mostly by their names. I pick a horse with a nice-sounding name, one that indicates he'll make an honest effort to win."

"All right," Mason said, "now I'm going to ask you some questions. You must have been at the race track in order to place the bets and get the tickets?"

She hesitated a moment, then said, "Yes."

"And you left the racetrack before the race was run?"

Again she hesitated, then said, "Yes."

"So you now have no knowledge of whether this horse won or not?"

"That's right."

"But at odds of this sort your horse must have been pretty well down in the cat-and-dog division."

"I would assume so. Really, Mr. Mason, these matters are all so obvious. Is it necessary to take my limited time to go over all this? Can't you take it for granted that all of these things are so?"

4

"I just wanted to let you know that I had them in mind," Mason said, "because I am now going to ask you *why* you left the racetrack before the race was run? In making a bet of this size, you must have burned a lot of bridges. You took a desperate gamble, even assuming that you had some very accurate advance information. The winning of these bets certainly means a lot to you."

"You may also take that for granted."

"Then *why* did you leave the racetrack?"

"That," she said, "is something I don't have the time to discuss at the present moment. I am asking you please to act as my attorney. I want you to collect this money for me. I have here twenty dollars as a retainer. In the event the horse has won, I will make adjustments with you covering compensation for the time you have used in going to the racetrack and collecting on the tickets.

"In the event the horse has not won, there is nothing for you to do except toss the tickets in the wastebasket. In that event you have twenty dollars for the time you have given me."

"How do I get in touch with you—if I get the money?" Mason asked.

"I'll get in touch with you."

"When?"

"Tomorrow. Is there a number where I can reach you?"

"Tomorrow is Saturday. The office won't be open. The Drake Detective Agency with offices on this floor is open twenty-four hours a day. Call that number and ask for Paul Drake. He can always reach me.

"However, if the horse should win, I don't want to be carrying a whole wad of currency around with me. I could deposit it and get a cashier's check—"

"No checks," she interrupted. "Cash. No bills larger than a hundred dollars. There shouldn't be much risk to a big man like you. I suppose you have a permit to carry a gun."

"I have a permit," Mason said.

"Better use it then," she said, her eyes twinkling. "I'd

dislike having you held up and relieved of my money. Be careful."

She rose abruptly, flashed him a dazzling smile, said, "Thank you very much, Mr. Mason," turned, gave her hand to Della Street and said, "You've been *so* kind and considerate, Miss Street, I certainly appreciate it."

With that, she swept across the office to the exit door, opened it and started out into the corridor.

"Just a moment," Mason said, "I want to . . ."

His words were lost in the closing of the door.

"Shall I get her back?" Della asked.

Mason smiled and shook his head. "We'll ask her when we see her again."

"You think you'll see her again?"

Mason nodded.

"How much chance does that horse stand of winning?" Della Street asked.

"The horse," Mason said, "has already won."

"What makes you think so?"

"She didn't leave the racetrack," Mason said, "until after the race had been run. She's too excited, too keyed up—and I don't think there's any power on earth except personal danger that could have dragged her from the racetrack after she had placed five hundred dollars in bets on the nose of a horse that was estimated to pay odds of fifty to one."

"There's a broadcast of the races at five-thirty," Della Street said. "It's very realistic. They tape it right at the track and then broadcast it on the radio later on. We can listen and find out what horse won."

"We can listen," Mason said, "but I'll now give you odds that Dough Boy won the race."

Della Street raised inquiring eyebrows. "You're that certain?"

Mason said, "The bets had to be placed at the track. The bets couldn't be placed until after the previous race had been completed. So we have our mysterious client placing five hundred dollars on a horse that is down pretty much at

6

the foot of the list. Now, can you imagine any circumstances which would cause her to leave the track before that race was run?"

"Nothing short of a murder," Della Street admitted.

Mason gave that remark frowning contemplation.

"Well?" she asked.

"I was going to say," Mason said, "that we could take it for granted that Dough Boy won the race; we could take it for granted that our client must have remained at the track until the result was certain and, for some reason best known to herself, doesn't dare to present the winning tickets at the window. I was going to add that we could clinch our theory by pointing out that a young woman in moderate circumstances would hardly go to a lawyer's office and pay twenty dollars to have him made the custodian of losing horse-race tickets.

"Moreover, if something had happened and our client had had to leave the track before the race was run, she would have saved herself twenty dollars by waiting until the results of the race were broadcast and *then* going to the attorney . . . only by that time law offices could be closed—this is Friday afternoon."

"All that is so logical," Della Street said, "that you've convinced me"

"The trouble is," Mason told her, "this is all on a take-it-for-granted basis. One of the most dangerous things anyone can do in the practice of law is to take things for granted."

The telephone rang and Della answered. After a moment, she replaced its receiver, turned to Mason and said, "It appears your four o'clock appointment has been held up, so may I suggest we work on correspondence until five-thirty and then tune in the race broadcast?"

Mason nodded.

Della smiled. "I'm glad we're going to get some of this correspondence caught up," she said. "It's high time."

Mason opened a file marked with a red sticker, URGENT,

picked up a letter, scanned it briefly, tossed it to Della Street, said, "Write this man that I'm not interested."

He read the next letter, handed it to her, said, "Tell this man I've got to know more about the circumstances of the case and particularly about the witness who made the positive identification."

Della Street took each letter as Mason handed it to her, made shorthand notes indicating the nature of the reply, and by five-fifteen they had cleaned up the urgent pile of correspondence.

"There's another one that's not urgent but is rather important," Della said.

Mason shook his head. "I've had enough correspondence for the night," he said. "I like to write letters to friends but I hate business letters. You write them, and then you get an answer. It's a treadmill operation. The answers come in as fast as the letters go out. You never get anywhere.

"Bring out the electric percolator, Della. We'll make some coffee. Give Paul Drake a ring and ask him if he wants to come on down the hall and join us for a cup of coffee. Tell him we're going to listen to a rebroadcast, or whatever it is, of the horse races."

Della nodded, moved over to the closet where they kept the electric coffee percolator, coffee cups, sugar and Pream; then telephoned Paul Drake.

"He's coming," she said. "He says he had a hot tip on the third race and managed to get a small bet down."

"The third?" Mason said. "That's the one Dough Boy is in."

Della nodded again.

"Now, wouldn't it be just too charming if it should turn out Paul Drake has a tip on Dough Boy to win?"

"Well," Della said, as Drake's knock sounded on the door, "here's the gambler now."

She opened the door and Drake said, "Hi, Beautiful. Why the sudden interest in horse races?"

Della looked in Perry Mason's direction and said, "No comment."

Mason grinned. "Just wanted to relax a bit, Paul. We get in a terrific grind here in the office. Our days become strait-jacketed into a pattern of come-to-the-office-in-the-morning, wrestle-with-telephone-calls-and-correspondence, dash-up-to-court-for-a-brief-hearing, then back-to-the-office-and-handle-correspondence and—"

"You're breaking my heart," Drake said, "but you haven't answered the question."

"How come *you're* interested in horse racing?" Mason asked.

"A hobby," Drake said. "I use it to take my mind off my business. I violate the law by patronizing a bookie. I can't get out to the track. Occasionally I get a hot tip. However, you're avoiding the question. How about *your* interest in horse racing?"

"Just a hobby," Mason said. "I use it as a means of relaxation, to get away from the arduous cares of my work."

"I should charge you a royalty," Drake said. "Going to have doughnuts to go with the coffee, Della?"

"Not unless you go down and buy some."

"I'll go," Drake said. "There's a place around the corner that specializes in fresh doughnuts. I'll get some with chocolate icing, powdered sugar and—"

"No chocolate icing for me," Della said.

"Nor me," Mason chimed in.

"Nor me," Drake agreed reluctantly. "I just like to talk big. . . . What's your horse, Perry?"

"One in the third race," Mason said, "a horse by the name of Dough Boy."

"Dough Boy!" Drake exclaimed.

Mason, watching his face closely, nodded.

Drake thew back his head and laughed.

"What's the trouble?" Mason asked.

"Dough Boy!" Drake exclaimed. "Good Lord, why

don't you donate your money to the track and be done with it? Why, Dough Boy doesn't stand a whisper of a chance. He won't be a quarter of the way around the track by the time the leader is finishing. Gee Whiz is the nag to bet on. Good Lord, Perry, don't tell me that you're playing some of these long-shot tips. They're a dime a dozen."

"I don't know much about it," Mason said modestly.

"I'll say you don't," Drake told him. "You've fallen for the oldest gag in racing. Now, listen to me and get some of the facts of life straight from the horse's mouth.

"There are all kinds of tips floating around. You can get good tips and bad tips. If you have a regular tipster and he knows you're acting on his tips, he tries to give you a winner. But if you aren't a regular customer and a tout feels that he can only get you once, he picks a long shot. Every time there's a long shot running some tout will pick a credulous bird who doesn't know anything about the track or about handicapping and give him a tip on that long shot. If it doesn't pay off, which it doesn't nine hundred and ninety-nine times out of a thousand, you never hear from the tout again. If it does pay off, he has you hooked but good and he's got a nice tip coming.

"The only way to pick a horse is on the basis of past performance, on the weight the nag is carrying, the condition of the track, and above all, the jockey who's riding him. . . . Tell me, Perry, who was this tipster? Someone you know?"

"No."

"A rather seedy-looking chap who—"

"A neatly dressed woman."

"A woman!"

"Right."

"A looker"

"And how."

"How old?"

"Twenty-five or six."

Drake roared with laughter. "Don't ever tell anyone else,

Perry! This is good. The shrewdest lawyer at the bar falling for a trick so old it has whiskers. You can bet that woman called on two dozen other suckers with the same tip. Being a good-looking babe she could get in to see people— Oh, Perry!"

Mason looked at his watch. "Thanks for your help, Paul. Now, if *we're* going to get those doughnuts before the broadcast starts . . ."

Drake grinned. "Meaning *I* had better get started. Okay, on my way."

Mason looked over at Della Street and smiled. "I think we can safely assume," he said, "that Paul Drake has *not* placed any money on Dough Boy."

Chapter 2

The voice of the announcer, droning the information, emerged from the loud-speaker. "In the third, they're away. It's a good start. They're running bunched together. Gee Whiz, the favorite, is going to the front on the outside. Hard Times is second. Deep End is third. Carte Blanche is fourth. Dough Boy is fifth. At the far turn it's Gee Whiz by a length. Deep End is second. Hard Times is third. Turning into the stretch it's Gee Whiz by a length. Deep End and Hard Times are running neck and neck in second place. Pot O'Gold leads Carte Blanche by a neck."

Drake grinned, pulled a chocolate-coated doughnut out of the bag and bit into it. "Looks like I've hit the jackpot," he said and then, after a moment, laughed. "Dough Boy!" he exclaimed. "This is really good."

The announcer went on. "Deep End is falling back. Dough Boy is coming fast from the rear. He's passed Carte Blanche, is passing Deep End, is gaining on Hard Times."

Drake slowly put down the chocolate-coated doughnut, lowered the coffee cup, glanced at Perry Mason.

"It's Gee Whiz and Hard Times running neck and neck, then Dough Boy. Deep End is a neck behind. Pot O'Gold is back a length. Then Carte Blanche. Hard Times passes Gee Whiz. It's Hard Times by a neck, Gee Whiz second, Dough Boy third. Dough Boy is creeping up. Dough Boy passes Gee Whiz. Dough Boy and Hard Times are running neck and neck. Dough Boy is ahead by a nose. At the finish, it's Dough Boy. Dough Boy, by a neck. Dough boy, first; Hard Times, second. Gee Whiz is third."

Della Street turned down the radio. "Finish your dough-nut, Paul."

Paul Drake said in a somewhat awed voice, "Well, I'll be damned."

He bit into the doughnut, added, "Leave that thing on, Della. Let's find out what the odds were. Good Lord, that nag must have been carrying the United States mint with him. Dough Boy—well, of all things! Why, the horse had no more business . . . winning— Can you beat that?"

Della Street turned up the radio and held her pencil poised over the paper waiting for the odds. When they came, she marked them down on a piece of paper, handed them to Mason.

Paul Drake shook his head and gave a low whistle. "Fifty-seven bucks for two!" he said. "That's twenty-seven and a half to one odds. Did you bet two bucks?"

Mason's smile was enigmatic. "I had more or less of an academic interest in the race, Paul."

"Fifty-seven dollars," Drake repeated slowly. "Lord, do you peasants know what that means? It means that if someone had had guts enough to make a hundred-dollar bet on Dough Boy, they'd be two thousand, seven hundred and fifty bucks to the good right now."

Drake shook his head, sighed wistfully and said, "Two thousand, seven hundred an fifty bucks. Even a fifty-dollar bet would have— "

"Well, how about a two-dollar bet?" Mason asked.

Drake grinned. "A two-dollar bet would have netted you fifty-five bucks. That would have paid all your expenses at the track, paid for a nice dinner by candlelight with champagne and a good-looking babe, a dance and . . ." Drake suddenly shook his head and said, "But I didn't have two bucks on him. I lost my two bucks on Gee Whiz. I'm eating a chocolate-coated doughnut. I suppose you and Della will go out and celebrate now."

"Not a bad idea, Della," Mason said. "Why don't we

dine by candlelight, with a nice filet mignon and a baked potato?"

"Because," she said, "my figure has severed diplomatic relations with the potato. Make it garden peas and it's a deal."

Drake sighed wistfully. "It's nice to listen to how the other half lives," he said, pushing back his cup and saucer. "Well, I have a whole stack of work to do in the office before I can call it a day. How did you get that tip, Perry?"

Della said, "It's a new system he has. He never seems to miss. He can pick them every time."

Drake's eyes widened.

Della continued, "He doesn't pay any attention to the odds or the weight, the condition of the track, or who the jockey is. He simply looks down the list of the horses and picks out the one whose name he likes—a horse that will make an honest effort to win. Now, Dough Boy has a nice name. There's something solid about it, something that— "

"Oh, my God!" Drake exclaimed in disgust. "You amateurs! You'll go broke playing a system like that. You don't stand a whisper of a chance."

"I know," Mason said. "How did you pick Gee Whiz, Paul?"

"Scientifically—on the basis of past performances, the showing he— Oh, go to hell. Rub it in! But your fifty-five bucks will go down the drain fast with the system *you're* using."

Mason carelessly produced the five one-hundred-dollar tickets. "I hate piker bets," he said. "These represent five hundred bucks right on the nag's nostrils."

Drake looked at the tickets in stupefied amazement, then said almost reverently, "Over fourteen thousand smackers!"

He raised his eyes to the lawyer's face.

"Perry, you didn't— Well, now I've seen everything!"

The detective jerked the door open. "An honest effort," he said, "a nice-sounding name— Hell!"

He shot out of the door.

Mason grinned at Della Street.

"Well," she said, "where do we go from here?"

"To dinner," Mason said, "and to the track tomorrow afternoon. There's a window where they pay off on the previous day's winners. I'll show up with five one-hundred-dollar tickets. According to Drake's figures, that entitles me to— How much, Della?"

Della Street made rapid marks with the pencil. "A slight matter of fourteen thousand, two hundred and fifty dollars," she said. "That includes the original five hundred that was bet."

"That," Mason told her, "would be quite a windfall for a young secretary who is out of work and is trying to get someone to share the expenses of her apartment. . . . I have also heard that the Bureau of Internal Revenue keeps a representative on hand to check the names and addresses of the people who make big winnings."

"How nice," Della said. "A one-man reception committee. I take it you'll want a witness."

"Oh, definitely," Mason said.

"And we have to go to the track to collect in person."

"That's right," Mason told her. "The urgent correspondence is all caught up. We'd better take a brief case to put the money in."

"Would you," Della Street asked, "mind picking a horse for me to bet on tomorrow? Just one with a good, substantial name; one that seems to be the sort of horse that would make an honest effort."

"Not at all," Mason told her. "It will be a pleasure."

Chapter 3

Mason inched his way through the congested traffic approaching the parking spaces at the racetrack, finally found a parking space, helped Della Street out of the car, and together they approached the grandstand.

"Did you pick me a horse?" Della asked. "A horse with a nice substantial name? A horse that will do his best?"

"I've picked him," Mason said.

"Which one is it?" she asked.

"His name," Mason said, "is Pound Sterling. Doesn't that sound like money in the bank?"

"Oh, wonderful," she exclaimed. "What do I do about it?"

Mason gravely handed her two dollars. "You go to the betting window as soon as it opens," he said, "hand the man two dollars and tell him you want to bet on number six. That is the number of Pound Sterling."

"Two dollars?" Della Street said. "With a name like that, and a horse that's selected by the great Perry Mason? Two dollars would be an insult! I'm going to bet ten dollars."

"Now look," Mason told her, "a gag's a gag, but ten dollars is ten dollars."

"Pound Sterling isn't a gag," she told him. "It's money in the bank. The name rings a bell."

"A two-dollar bell," Mason said.

"Ten dollars."

"Two."

"Look here, suppose he wins and you've talked me out of making a ten-dollar bet, *then* how would you feel?"

Mason sighed. "Arguing with a woman is a waste of time. Make it ten."

"Ten it is," she said.

They found seats in the grandstand. The windows opened on the first race; Della Street returned from the ten-dollar window with a ticket on Pound Sterling. "Right on his nose," she said.

"Well," Mason told her, "we may as well get our business obligations over with. I'll go to the window which pays off on bets made yesterday and present the tickets. You stand by as a witness to any conversation that may take place."

"Do they indulge in conversation?" Della Street asked.

"The man at the window doesn't" Mason said, "but someone else may."

"What someone?"

"The someone our client wished to avoid," Mason told her. "Come on, let's go."

Della Street said, "Would it be a good idea for me to take one of the tickets and approach the window first and you could stand in the background and size the situation up?"

Mason shook his head. "We're going to have to cash the tickets. Those are instructions from our client. We may as well do it all at once, and I may as well be the one who does it. Then if there's any trouble I'll try to make it look as natural as possible and not give anyone a chance to say I had some guilty knowledge, and for that reason was trying to work through you and to cash one ticket at a time."

"If anything happens, do I pretend that I don't know you and stand to one side?"

"No," Mason said, "we don't pretend anything. You're my secretary, you're here with me normally and naturally. We're enjoying the races this afternoon and cashing in on bets we made yesterday."

"Bet's *we* made?" she asked.

"That would be the natural assumption."

"Do we implement it with conversation?"

"We implement it with nothing," Mason said. "We pick up the booty and walk away. There may be a representative of the Bureau of Internal Revenue inquiring about my name and address."

"You'll give him that information?"

"My name and address—certainly."

They walked in silence to the window which was paying off past bets. Mason produced the five tickets, pushed them through the window.

The man looked at the tickets, looked at Mason, said, "Third race yesterday, number four, right on the nose."

Mason nodded.

"How do you want this?" the man asked. "Any objection to large bills?"

"No objection," Mason said, "but nothing bigger than hundreds."

The man started counting out currency, shoved the pile of bills across to Mason. "There you are," he said.

Mason picked up the money, opened his brief case.

A rather short man in his early fifties, with a sallow complexion, sharp gimlet eyes and a nervous manner, rushed forward.

"There he is!" he shouted. "That's him. Arrest him!"

An easy-moving, broad-shouldered individual came lumbering in the wake of the excited little man, produced a leather folder, opened it and showed the badge.

"Police," he said.

"Mind if I look?" Mason asked. He took the leather container and the badge from the man's hand, held it so Della Street could see the number on the badge, said, "all right, you're police."

"Where'd you get those tickets?" the officer asked.

"He knows where he got them. He got them from Rodney Banks, and it's my money," the smaller man shouted.

"Shut up," the officer said.

Mason turned to the officer. "Perhaps you'd like one of my cards."

18

He handed the officer a card.

The officer looked at it. "Perry Mason, huh? Thought your face was familiar. I should have placed you. I've seen pictures of you in the newspapers."

"The money," the excitable little man said. "The money—get the money, Officer. Don't let him talk you out of the money."

"Shut up," the officer said.

Mason turned to the excited individual. "My name's Mason," he said, smiling down. "Who are you?"

"You know good and well who I am," the man said. "I'm Marvin Fremont."

"And just what makes you think you're entitled to *this* money, Mr. Fremont?" Mason asked.

"You know good and well why I'm entitled to it. That money came from a bet made by Rodney Banks, and the five hundred dollars he bet was embezzled from me. Now then, Officer, I want my money."

The officer hesitated.

"Go ahead, take it. Take him into custody. He's an accomplice," Fremont shouted.

Mason grinned at the hesitant officer. "What's your name?" he asked.

"Sid Burdett."

Mason extended his hand.

The two shook hands.

"Now, I'm investigating an alleged theft or embezzlement," the officer said. "I guess there's no question but what this man, Banks, bet the money, and it looks very much as though Banks had been dipping into the till. He works for Marvin Fremont, here. That is, he did work for him."

"Go ahead, get busy! Take the money away from him," Fremont said to the officer. "That's what *you're* here for. He's an accomplice. Arrest him and throw him in with the other one. Some crooked lawyer in cahoots with an embezzler. The same old— Hey, Officer, she's taking notes."

"I noticed," Burdett said.

"My secretary," Mason explained.

"What's she taking notes for?"

"I have just been called a crooked lawyer in the presence of witnesses," Mason said. "I feel that gives me a cause of action against this *gentleman,* here."

"What are you talking about, a cause of action?" Fremont said. "If anybody has a cause of action, I've got it. My money was used in making this bet."

Burdett said to Mason, "I take it Rodney Banks is your client?"

"Don't take things for granted," Mason told him.

"You mean he isn't?"

"I didn't say that either," Mason said.

"Well," Burdett said, "I'm investigating, that's all. This Rodney Banks is in jail charged with embezzlement. He evidently had been betting on the horses and got in pretty deep. Then he got a hot tip on Dough Boy in yesterday's race, and I guess he really went to town and cleaned out the till to make the bet. However, Fremont was wise to what was going on by that time, so he got here at the racetrack to make the arrest."

"Who made the arrest?" Mason asked.

"I did," Burdett said. "We couldn't find the guy, but we saw Dough Boy come in a heavy winner so we went over to the pay-off windows and started looking around. Sure enough, Banks came up to the fifty-dollar window, presented a fifty-dollar ticket, and just before he was paid off I made the pinch."

"He make any statements?" Mason asked.

"Denied everything and then clammed."

"You searched him?"

"Sure, I searched him. Frisked him for a gun when I made the pinch and then of course at the jail we took everything out of his clothes."

"No tickets?"

"No tickets. Just that one fifty-buck ticket was all."

"And you thought there were more?"

"We were pretty sure there were more. He'd evidently slipped the tickets to some accomplice."

Mason turned to Fremont. "How much is the amount of the embezzlement, Mr. Fremont?"

"I don't know," Fremont said.

"Why don't you know?"

"It's all mixed up."

"How is it all mixed up?"

"The bankbooks. Money has been juggled," Fremont said. "I'm going to have an audit. But I know one thing, all that money is my money. It makes no difference how much is *missing*. The five hundred dollars came out of my business and it's stolen money. I still own it."

Mason said thoughtfully, "Perhaps Banks won enough to be able to make good all the shortages; provided, of course, there were any shortages, and I am now referring to the money he won on his fifty-dollar ticket."

"It's not his money, it's mine," Fremont said. "I guess I know a little law myself. That's *my* money. I have the title to it. He embezzled it. That doesn't make it *his* money, it's still *my* money. He bet it on a horse and he gets lucky. That doesn't change the picture at all as far as I'm concerned. He's in my employ and it's my money and those are my winnings."

"You," Mason told him, "had better see a lawyer."

"I've seen a lawyer."

"Then you'd better ask him some more questions," Mason said.

"You arrest him," Fremont said, tapping Burdett on the sleeve. "He's an accomplice."

Burdett shook his head. "I'm not arresting this man. He's a lawyer."

"And," Mason said to Fremont, "after you consult your lawyer, ask him what he thinks of my chances of recovering damages."

"Damages?"

21

"You called me a crooked lawyer," Mason explained.

Burdett grinned.

Fremont said, "Why, you . . . you . . . shyster!"

"Got that down, Della?" Mason asked.

She nodded.

"Della Street, my secretary, gentlemen," Mason said.

Burdett turned to Fremont. "Okay, Mr. Fremont," he said. "He called the turn. You see a lawyer."

"All right," Fremont said, "I've got a lawyer, and a private detective, and I wish to hell I'd relied on them instead of you. It was the lawyer that told me to have an officer here and have the accomplice arrested.

"Now I'll tell both of you something. If this money gets away from me, I'm going to hold both of you responsible."

"Do that," Mason said.

There was a great uproar from the track. Someone shouted, "They're off!"

Mason and Della Street moved away from Fremont and the officer, hurried over to where they could see the running horses circling the track.

"What a wonderful, magnetic personality," Della Street said.

"Not bad, as bosses go," Mason told her. "I just wanted to remind you, Miss Street, that you are working for a veritable paragon of employers."

She laughed and squeezed his arm. "The job does have *some* compensations. Now, if you can just root for Pound Sterling and bring him in . . ."

"With a name like that," Mason said, "he couldn't lose."

They stood watching the horses come down the home stretch to the finish.

Pound Sterling wasn't even in the money.

"And with a name like that," Della Street said.

"Well, let's try one in the next race," Mason said. "Now, you've had your fill of horses with good, worthy names who could be counted on to make an honest effort. Let's try a thoroughly disreputable horse. Here's one in the second race, Counterfeit Cash. Now *there's* a horse who should put up a thoroughly reprehensible performance."

"Two dollars on the nose," Della Street said.

Mason said, "Give me the money for the bet and I'll place it for you, Della."

Mason went to the ten-dollar window. "Pound Sterling didn't do so good for us," he said. "How about number five, Counterfeit Cash?"

"One?"

"Two," Mason said. "Two ten-dollar tickets, right on the nose."

The man at the window took the currency, handed Mason two tickets.

Mason rejoined Della Street in the grandstand.

"Don't you feel you need an armed escort with all that money you're carrying?" she asked.

"It's quite a roll," Mason admitted, "and we may be in for trouble. I'm now suspicious of everything and everybody."

"In what way?"

"I don't know," Mason said, "but it now appears that I'm mixed up in some way with an embezzler, that I'm holding currency about which there's a dispute, to say the least, and an attempt is being made to tag me as an accessory to an embezzlement. However, let's enjoy the races and then quietly get the hell out of here."

They watched the illuminated tote board.

"Estimated odds on Counterfeit Cash," Mason said, "are twenty to one. They should drop a little bit before the horses go to the starting gate."

"How come?" she asked.

"Long odds like that on a horse tempt people to make bets just for the odds. Usually they're small bets but there are quite a few people who, having lost ten two-dollar bets, look at a horse that is supposed to pay off at ten to one and will bet on the odds, just hoping they can break even."

Mason looked around the crowd in the grandstand, then

said in a low voice to Della Street, "Here's our friend, Marvin Fremont. He seems to be keeping us under what he would doubtless call surveillance."

"He doesn't want to take any chances on you getting reckless and betting his bankroll," she said.

"There's something mighty strange about the whole thing," Mason said.

"Oh-oh," Della Street said, "here go the odds. They're down to eighteen to one and now— Oh-oh, fifteen to one. I don't see how anyone would bet on a horse with a name like that unless they were people who got hooked on that Pound Sterling horse. Imagine a horse with a name like that not even getting in the money."

"Well," Mason said, "I think we'll get out of here and lock this money in our safe."

"But we're going to see this race?" Della Street asked.

"Very definitely we're going to see this race," Mason said. "I wouldn't want *you* to have to retain a lawyer to cash in *your* ticket."

Della Street laughed.

Mason handed her the ticket, said, "This time we'll keep an eye on the horse and see if we can coax him along to victory."

They chatted for a few moments, then Della Street said, "There's your man standing over there and this time he has two others with him."

Mason glanced over his shoulder, said, "He's probably sent for reinforcements."

"What can he do?" she asked.

"Not a darned thing," Mason said.

"Suppose the money was embezzled?"

"We don't know a thing about it," Mason said, "and what's more, no one else does. There's no way on earth those tickets can be identified. Of course, the man at the betting window might happen to remember the *person* who made such a bet on a long shot. He probably would, but he can't identify the money."

24

"And suppose it turns out that the person who made the bet is the embezzler?" Della Street asked.

"Then," Mason said, "they have to do several things. They have to prove that he bought the tickets with embezzled money. They have to prove that he came to me, that I acted as his agent, or that I knew the money was embezzled. Then they have to go to court to get the money."

"Unless they should arrest you," Della Street said, "in which event the money would be impounded at the jail."

"In which event," Mason said, "this man, Fremont, whoever he is, would find that he'd stirred up a lot more action than he'd bargained for. And then of course he'd find himself confronted with the same problems, only then, in a criminal case, they'd have to prove each point beyond all reasonable doubt and not just by a preponderance of the evidence. . . . They're off, Della."

"Which one is ours?"

"Number five," Mason said.

"Oh-oh," Della said, "he's back third, he's drifting back fourth. . . . I'm afraid he didn't have an honest name and isn't making an effort—"

"Wait a minute," Mason said, "he's forging ahead now. He's coming up to third place."

Della Street said, "He's got to do a lot better than that. I bet right on the nose."

"Well, he's bringing his nose along," Mason said. "He's running even with the third now. Wait a minute, they're rounding the turn, he's passed the horse in third place, he's coming up on second— Come on, number five, come on!" Mason shouted.

Number five inched up on the horse in second place, then nosed up on the favorite as they ran in a tight group down the home stretch.

The crowd became suddenly silent. Then hundreds of voices started rooting for the favorite.

Della jumped up on the seat, her hands on Mason's

shoulders, "Come on, come on, come on!" she shouted. "Oh, Chief, I believe he's going to— No, he didn't."

She settled down dejectedly, then said, "Gosh, if I'd only thought to put a two-dollar bet on him in second place, I could have won."

"It's a photo finish," Mason said. "It was that close. They're going to have to develop the picture."

"How long will that take?"

"Not long," Mason said. "We'll ease our way toward the exit and be ready to go as soon as we hear the result."

"You mean there's a chance?"

"A good chance," Mason said. "At least an even-money chance."

"An even-money chance on odds of fifteen to one," Della Street said. "Good grief, that'll be something. Why don't we stay for the rest of the races? Maybe we can—"

"You're forgetting," Mason said, "this is business. You're getting the fever."

They moved toward the exit.

"Well, here's our reception committee," Della Street said.

Marvin Fremont pushed forward. "You said I should get a lawyer? I've got a lawyer."

One of the men said, "I'm Bannister Dowling, Mr. Mason. I'm representing Marvin Fremont."

"Good," Mason said. "He'll need you."

"And this is Moray Hobart, of the Hobart Detective Agency.'

"A private detective, I take it?" Mason asked.

"Right," Hobart said.

"All right," Mason said, "I have only a few moments. What do you people want?"

"Money," Hobart said. "And we want it now, Mr. Mason."

"You've got some money that belongs to my client," Dowling explained.

26

"What makes you think it belongs to your client?" Mason asked.

Hobart said, "The money was bet on the horse yesterday."

"What horse?" Mason asked.

"Dough Boy."

"And that makes the money belong to Marvin Fremont?" Mason asked.

Dowling said, "We may just as well understand each other, Mason. Rodney Banks embezzled money from my client in order to make a bet on a long shot. He was short in his accounts and he wanted to pay off. Getting a long-shot bet was the only chance he had. . . . By that time we were on to him. Moray Hobart spotted him at the fifty-dollar window collecting a bet on Dough Boy. We surmised he also had some other bets on the horses."

"Then what did he do with the tickets?" Mason asked.

"He gave them to an accomplice, and the accomplice gave them to you," Dowling said.

"And who was the accomplice?"

"His sister. She was seen at the hundred-dollar window."

"Why didn't you arrest her?"

"Because she didn't show up to cash in on her winnings. Her brother's arrest frightened her. She got away from us."

"You can identify the money she bet?" Mason asked.

"Almost. We haven't all the bill numbers."

"Very interesting," Mason said. "I fail to see how it concerns me."

Dowling said, "If the money was embezzled, Banks had no title to it, and if he had no title to it, any money that he won automatically became the property of my client. In other words, he didn't have title to the money, he had only the physical possession of the money and he was holding it in trust. Any increment belongs to my client."

"This is a very interesting situation," Mason said. "I want to be sure that I get your point of view. Banks was an embezzler?"

27

"Yes."

"But the money that he had won would have covered his shortage?"

"I believe," Dowling said, "I'm not violating any confidence in stating that it would have more than covered the shortage."

"But Banks is in jail?"

"He's arrested on a charge of embezzlement. The bail is five thousand dollars. So far he hasn't been able to raise it."

"And I take it the embezzlement was for less than five thousand dollars?"

"Actually it was."

"Then you have no intention of letting him make restitution?"

"Certainly not. That would be compounding a felony. My client intends to hold him for the embezzlement."

"And at the same time to take the winnings on the bet?"

"Certainly. The money is my client's."

"Well, it's an interesting theory," Mason said. "I'm sorry, but I can't subscribe to the theory and——"

"You can at least tell us how you came into possession of the tickets," Dowling said.

Mason merely smiled.

"I want you to understand," Dowling said, "that we're going to be fair with you and courteous with you, Mr. Mason. As a matter of professional courtesy, I'm going to give you every opportunity to co-operate. But in view of the facts that I have stated to you now, you're placed on notice of the true situation and you can become an accessory after the fact as far as the embezzlement is concerned, and an accomplice of the embezzler."

"Thank you," Mason said. "I'm afraid I don't need to have you tell me the law. I have an office full of lawbooks and I can look it up in case I don't know it."

"All right," Dowling said angrily, "go look up the question of what makes a man an accessory after the fact, and don't kid yourself that just because you're a lawyer you can get away with helping an embezzler."

"And the reason I suggested to your client that he consult a lawyer," Mason said, "was because he made defamatory statements in the presence of witnesses. He called me a shyster and a crooked lawyer."

Dowling looked at Fremont.

"That's a lie," Fremont said. "That's absolutely not so. Mr. Mason misunderstood me. I was talking about something else entirely, about other lawyers."

"About Mr. Dowling?" Mason asked.

"Don't let him trap you," Dowling said, holding up his hand with the palm toward Fremont's mouth. "Don't say a word. Shut up right now. You've said enough."

"Too much," Mason said.

"There's some witness?" Dowling asked Mason.

"My secretary," Mason said, "and an officer, whose name I believe is Sidney Burdett."

"His secretary," Fremont snorted. "She'd say anything to—"

"Shut up," Dowling commanded.

"Let him keep talking," Mason said. "Perhaps my secretary will also have a cause of action."

"I think," Dowling said, "we'll carry on this discussion in the absence of my client."

"You'll carry it on in my absence also," Mason said. "We're just waiting for . . ."

Lights flashed on the board. The voice of an announcer said, "The photo finish gives the first place in the race to number five, Counterfeit Cash, second place to Bigger and Better; third place Hot Head."

Mason turned to Della Street. "Let's go cash our tickets, Della, and be on our way. Or do you also claim *these* winnings as well as the others?"

"Say, wait a minute," Fremont said. "What kind of a system are you using?"

"It's a very simple system," Mason said, "and it's virtually infallible."

"What is it?" Fremont asked, his eyes alight with interest.

"Suppose you let me do the talking," Dowling said.

Mason smiled at the attorney. "I was about to answer your client's question, but since you prefer that I don't talk with him, and that he doesn't talk with me, I think it's better to preserve the ethics of the situation. Come on, Della."

"Hey, wait a minute!" Fremont said. "He didn't mean not to talk about horse racing. He meant not to talk about what I said—I mean, what you said I said . . . what— "

"*Will* you keep quiet?" Dowling asked.

Mason took Della Street's arm, led her to the cashier windows.

Della exerted gentle pressure against Mason's guiding arm. "It's this way, Chief," she said.

"No, it isn't," Mason said. "It's this way. Take a look at your ticket."

"Ten dollars!" Della Street exclaimed. "Why, you must have given me *your* ticket."

"No, I have one too," Mason said. "I thought we had worked out an almost infallible system, and I decided to go a little heavy on it. I hate to have you bet ten dollars on a loser and then only bet two dollars on a winner."

"Why, Chief, the odds are—"

"On your ten-dollar ticket," Mason said, "you will collect approximately— Well, let's see what you do collect."

Mason presented the tickets at the window, received one hundred and sixty dollars on each ticket.

"There you are, Della," he said. "Not bad for an afternoon at the track."

Fremont's voice sounded behind them. "Look here, now, Mr. Mason. We can be friends. I'd like to know how you pick horses."

"It's an infallible system," Mason said. "I promised the management of the track that I wouldn't divulge it to anyone, except a close personal friend, and you hardly qualify as a close personal friend. Come on, Della."

Mason escorted Della to the parked car.

"Don't make a point of it, Della," he said, "but turn to say something to me and look out of the corner of your eye, see if we're being followed."

Della Street turned to look at him, smiled brightly, nodded her head, and said, "You want me to turn and get a good look? I think it's that detective."

"No," Mason said, "we'll give the detective a merry chase."

They reached Mason's car. Mason handed Della Street in, got behind the steering wheel, slammed the door, stepped on the starter, and moved along at a snail's pace until he entered traffic. Then he began to speed up, watching from time to time in the rearview mirror.

He shot through a traffic signal just as it was changing, ran a block, turned to the left, turned to the right, then to the left again, then made a U-turn, doubled back and at length parked in a residential side street.

"Anything coming, Della?" he asked.

"Not a thing," she said. "It's all calm and serene. Did you think they were going to stick you up?"

"It's possible," Mason told her. "They'll probably have an operative staked out at your apartment and one at my office. They'll have trouble finding out where my apartment is so they can't pick up my trail there."

"So what do we do?"

"First," Mason said, "we avoid doing the obvious. We don't go to the office and we don't go to your apartment."

"But you're carrying all this cash," Della Street said.

"As well as a gun," Mason said, regarding her gravely. "Now, when an attorney has taken his secretary out to the races on a Saturday afternoon and has given her a tip on a long shot that pays off a hundred and sixty dollars on a ten-dollar bet, it would certainly seem that the situation would call for at least a reasonable celebration; something,

31

let us say, with steak—an extra-thick, medium-rare steak, French-fried onions, some champagne, and perhaps a little dancing."

"I think," she said, "you have the situation sized up perfectly. But what about our client?"

"Our client," Mason said, "is undoubtedly making an attempt to get in touch with us. We will check with Paul Drake now, and during the course of the evening we will call him again. By the time we start celebrating we should have been relieved of what I may call our cash responsibilities."

"She'll be wanting the money in the form of cash?" Della Street asked.

"Exactly," Mason said. "So we have to keep the money with us until we make a delivery."

"And you've now been notified the money was embezzled. Where does that leave you?"

"I have only been notified a man named Rodney Banks is accused of embezzlement. I must, however, give him the benefit of presuming he is innocent until he has been proven guilty.

"I don't know any Rodney Banks. No one has said Audrey Bicknell has embezzled anything. So, Miss Street, let us forget dull care."

"And the brief case with all the money?" she asked.

"In due time I will transfer the currency to a money belt and fill this brief case with newspapers. Does that answer your question?"

"It answers my question, but how about our client? Why is she anxious to get her money in cash and what will she do with it after she gets it?"

"Those are matters on which our client didn't choose to enlighten us, Della."

"Won't it be dangerous for her to carry a large sum of cash around with her?"

"She probably faces other dangers as well. We'll call Paul Drake and report, then we'll see what happens."

Chapter 4

From a phone booth Mason called Paul Drake's office and when he had the detective on the line, said, "Perry, Paul. How about messages for me? Do you have any?"

"Do I *have* any?" Drake said. "What is this fatal fascination that you have for women?"

"How come?"

"A seductive feminine voice, answering to the name of Audrey Bicknell, has called four times within the last hour and a half, asking if I have been in touch with you and giving a message I am to relay to you, which is of the utmost importance."

"What's the message?" Mason asked.

"Call the Foley Motel and ask for Miss Nancy Banks."

"Right away?" Mason asked.

"I'll say, right away. She's been biting pieces out of the mouthpiece on the telephone. She says it's important that she get in touch with you at the *very earliest* possible moment."

"Okay," Mason said, "I'll phone her."

"Right now?" Drake asked.

"I'm in a phone booth," Mason said. "It's a little noisy, but—"

"I have an idea it's pretty damned important, Perry. She certainly thinks so."

"Okay, I'll call," Mason said. "I'll check with you later. Be good."

The lawyer hung up the phone, called the Foley Motel and said, "I'd like to talk with Miss Nancy Banks, please."

"Just a moment. She's in Unit 14. Just hold on, please, I'll ring."

After a moment Mason heard a quick, eager voice on the telephone. "Hello. Hello. Mr. Mason?"

"Speaking," Mason said.

"I thought you'd *never* call. You went to the track?"

"Yes."

"You collected the money?"

"What money?" Mason asked.

"You know what money, Mr. Mason. The money for the tickets I gave you— Oh, I forgot, I gave you a different name when I was calling you. I said my name was Audrey Bicknell."

"Was that an alias?" Mason asked.

"Not an alias," she said. "Don't use that word. It was a pen name."

"All right, you're Nancy Banks," Mason said. "Now, what do you want?"

"Mr. Mason, I want you to take the money— Did you get the money all right?"

"Before I answer your question," Mason said, "you'd better finish your sentence. You started to tell me that you wanted me to take the money and—"

"That's right. I want you to go and put up bail for my brother, Rodney Banks. He's in jail charged with embezzlement, and bail has been fixed at five thousand dollars. Out of the money that you have collected from winnings on the horse, you can put up five thousand dollars and then bring the balance to me."

"Now, wait a minute," Mason said. "Things are coming pretty fast here, and you're getting your sequence all mixed up. So far you are just a voice over a telephone. Voices over a telephone are a dime a dozen.

"Now, if you're in a hurry, I'll arrange to meet with you at the most convenient place. You'll then identify yourself as the person who gave me the tickets. I'll then turn the money over to you and you'll give me a receipt for it. Then,

34

if you want me to put up bail for Rodney Banks, you give me the instructions in writing, give me the money to put up the bail and I'll put it up."

"That's going to consume a lot of time, Mr. Mason. Aren't you being unduly cautious?"

"I'm a lawyer," Mason said. "I'm dealing with a stranger. Under those circumstances, there isn't any such thing as being *unduly* cautious. Let's simply put it that I'm cautious, period."

"Very well," she said. "If that's the way you want to do it I guess you'll have to come out here to the motel. I'm . . . I'm hardly in a position to go out at the present time. I've been—I'm just out of the shower. I can be decent by the time you get here, however, and that's about the only way I can handle things. I can't save much time otherwise."

"I'll be right out," Mason said. "It will take me probably half an hour to get there."

"I'll be waiting. Tell me, did you have any trouble?"

"Nothing to speak of," Mason said. "I'll tell you all about it when I see you."

"Did anyone try to stop you?"

"From doing what?"

"Getting the money."

"Yes."

"Did you get it?"

"I'll explain the situation when I see you," Mason said. "But if you're the person who called at my office, you have nothing to worry about—as yet."

"Oh, Mr. Mason, I'm *so* glad—*so* thankful. I was *so* afraid, I—You'll be right out?"

"I'll be right out."

"Alone?"

"No," Mason said. "I'll have my secretary with me. She'll be a witness. I'm going to play this pretty close to my chest."

"All right," she said, laughing lightly. "Go ahead and be

as cautious as you want to. I don't suppose I can blame you."

"Thirty minutes," Mason said, and hung up.

It was exactly twenty-nine minutes later that the lawyer turned in at the motel. He drove to Unit 14, stopped and helped Della Street out of the car.

The door of Unit 14 opened.

The girl who had given him the name of Audrey Bicknell stood in the doorway. She wore a silk at-home costume of vibrant pink tight-fitting pants with a print jacket of pink and green, embroidered in crystal, which weighted the fine silk so that it hung to every curve above the hips.

"Come in, come in," she said, and smiling at Della Street, said, "It's a pleasure to see you again, Miss Street. Do come in."

Mason picked up his brief case from the car, entered the building.

"Did you get it?" she asked.

"I got it," Mason said. "Fourteen thousand, two hundred and fifty dollars." The lawyer opened the brief case, started counting money out on the table.

"Oh!" she exclaimed, as she saw the stacks of currency. "I had no idea it—It *is* a pile, isn't it, Mr. Mason?"

Mason nodded, kept on counting, stacking the money into piles of a thousand dollars each.

"All right," he said, "there you are. Sign this receipt that you've received the money from me, that it was all the money that was due you or was to become due you in return for some horse-race tickets that you gave me, and covers in full a collection that I was retained to make for you."

"You'll want your fee out of it, Mr. Mason," she said.

"That's right," Mason told her. "First we'll get all the money turned over to you. Then you'll pay me my fee."

"Can you tell me how much it is?"

"I can," Mason said, " but a little is going to depend on what you want me to do in connection with Rodney Banks. That is going to take a retainer, and I'm not in a position to tell you that I'll represent him on the embezzlement charge. I'm willing to put up the bail, acting as *your* attorney, but I'm not going to put myself in a position where I become obligated to act as *his* attorney—not until I know more about the case."

"Well, I can't blame you for that. I guess Rod was— Well, I guess he was pretty indiscreet. Even so, I simply *can't* reconcile the things he's supposed to have done. I think there's something in the background."

"All right," Mason said, "let's dispose of one thing at a time. Sign this receipt."

She signed the receipt Della Street handed her.

"Now," Mason said, "you want me to put up bail for Rodney Banks?"

"Yes, please."

"When?"

"Just as soon as you can possibly do it."

"Bail has been fixed?"

"Yes, he was taken before a magistrate. Bail was fixed at an amount of five thousand dollars cash."

Mason said, "You could have gone to a bail bond company and—"

"I know, I know, but they charge you for the risk involved and I didn't have the money."

Mason eyed her shrewdly. "But you *did* have five hundred dollars to bet on an almost hopeless long shot."

"He wasn't hopeless. He won."

"All right," Mason said, "we won't argue the point. Nothing succeeds like success. I'm going to charge you three hundred dollars for collecting the money. Then you'll give me five thousand for Rodney's bail. I'm going to charge you a hundred and fifty dollars for putting up the bail for him and I'll put it up in your name. I'll get a receipt for the five thousand bail made out to you. After that I'll have no further obligations in connection with the case."

"That's quite all right, Mr. Mason, quite all right. Here,

take the money, and— It's very important that we get him out this afternoon, Mr. Mason."

"Why?"

"Well, it's . . . it's important, that's all."

Mason said, "All right, we're dealing at arm's length. I'll give you a receipt for the five thousand, and for my fee."

Mason nodded to Della Street, who opened her notebook, wrote out a receipt, handed it to Mason for his inspection, and received a nod of approval; Mason scrawled his name on the bottom of the receipt, tore it out of Della Street's shorthand book, and handed it to the woman.

"Do I report to you here after I get him out?" Mason asked.

"No," she said. "It's better that you don't have any further contact with me. Tell me, did anyone try to follow you?"

"Yes," Mason said.

"But they didn't follow you here." Her voice was apprehensive.

"We took precautions to see that we weren't followed, up to the time I telephoned," Mason said. "You were in a hurry, so I didn't waste any time after I telephoned. I came here directly, but there's no indication anyone was following."

She nodded thoughtfully. "If anyone knew where I was, it would be . . . most inconvenient."

"And," Mason said, "you have a sizable chunk of currency there. You'd better see that it's put in a safe place."

"Yes, yes, I know. But you'll hurry, won't you, Mr. Mason? You'll get Rodney out."

"I'll put up the bail," Mason said, "and you don't want me to report?"

"No. We're . . . we're finished, Mr. Mason, and thank you very, very much indeed."

With an impulsive gesture she put her arms around him, hugged him briefly, then stepped back self-consciously.

"Okay," Mason said. "The next time you get a tip on any horses with nice honest-sounding names, who seem to be the type that can be depended upon to make an honest effort, just let me know."

The lawyer nodded to Della Street.

The woman who had given the name of Audrey Bicknell when she had called at Mason's office stood in the doorway watching them as they entered the car. Her expression was thoughtful and unsmiling.

"Well," Mason asked, as he eased the car out of the parking compartment, "what do you make of her, Della?"

"I don't know," Della Street said. "I guess she's Nancy Banks, all right; probably the sister of Rodney Banks, but she's certainly playing some game. She's just as taut as a fiddlestring and if you ask me she's frightened about something."

Chapter 5

Perry Mason, approaching the bail clerk at the jail, said, "You have a Rodney Banks charged with embezzlement, bail has been fixed at five thousand dollars cash, or a ten-thousand-dollar bond. I am Perry Mason, an attorney. I am putting up five thousand dollars cash on behalf of my client, Nancy Banks. Will you make a receipt to Nancy Banks for bail in an amount of five thousand dollars cash, please, and arrange for the release of Rodney Banks."

The clerk carefully counted the five thousand dollars which Mason paid over, took out a receipt form with carbon-paper copies, said, "What's the address of Nancy Banks?"

"Care of Perry Mason," the lawyer said.

"We should have a street address."

"You can have the address of my office."

The clerk hesitated, then made out the receipt. "In case of cash bail I guess it's all right."

"Now," Mason said, "I want to wait for Banks to be released."

"Present your receipt covering bail and he'll be released," the clerk said.

"I want immediate action," Mason said.

"You'll get it. You've put up the money. We don't want to keep him and feed him any longer than necessary. The money will guarantee his appearance at the time of trial—at least it should."

"It should," Mason agreed.

It was, however, some twenty minutes later when the

jailer escorted Rodney Banks into the room where Mason was waiting.

"Hello, Banks," Mason said. "I'm Perry Mason. I was retained to get you out on bail. I've put up the bail. I'm not acting as your attorney."

"Well, somebody's got to act as my attorney," Banks said. "They've pulled a fast one on me. I mean, here at the jail."

"What did they do?"

"They stole the ticket that I had on the winning race horse."

"Now, wait a minute, wait a minute," the officer said. "Nobody stole anything. You've got an order of attachment there."

"How come?" Mason asked.

"This guy had a ticket on Dough Boy, number four in the third race yesterday, for fifty bucks."

"That's a winning horse. At track odds that ticket is worth fourteen hundred and twenty-five dollars," Banks said.

Mason looked at the officer.

"The ticket was in his things, all right, when he was taken into custody. We gave him a receipt for all his stuff."

"But you didn't give me the ticket back," Banks protested.

"We couldn't," the officer said. "The ticket has been impounded. It's in the custody of the court. There's a notice in your things there—case of Fremont versus Banks. Fremont claims you embezzled the money that you used in betting on the horse, and that you're holding the ticket in trust for him."

"I could get the winnings on that ticket and he wouldn't have a whisper of a claim," Banks said indignantly.

"All I know about it," the officer said, "is that the ticket is impounded by order of court. You can fight it out in a civil action."

"But that doesn't affect the charge of embezzlement?" Mason asked.

"Apparently not," the officer said. "That charge is still pending."

Banks said hotly, "All the old goat claims that he's short is a little over a thousand dollars, and if he's right, there's plenty of money to pay off every cent of it. But he's trying to get the winning ticket on the horse and *then* prosecute a charge of embezzlement also."

Mason said, "I don't think I'm going to act as your attorney, young man. I'm not your attorney now. I'm going to tell you one thing. You're out on bail. Get out of here. There's no question that you had the winning ticket in your possession at the time you were arrested. That was a fifty-dollar ticket. It shows on the personal property receipt. Now then, you have a copy of writ there that was served on the officers, calling on them to hold that ticket. The court is going to impound the money.

"You have a lawsuit with Fremont as to who owns the money, and in addition to that Fremont has you arrested for embezzlement.

"Now, you can see Fremont's position. If you use that money to pay off the amount he's claimed you embezzled and there's no shortage, then he might be liable for damages for false arrest and for falsely accusing you of embezzlement—all of which depends on proof and on the state of the books.

"If he can claim that you made a fifty-dollar bet on Dough Boy, that it was made with embezzled money, then you become the involuntary trustee for his benefit of any winnings that may have been received, so he's still entitled to consider a shortage of over a thousand dollars as an embezzlement and at the same time claim the winnings, amounting to fourteen hundred and twenty-five dollars."

"That's unjust. He can't eat his cake and have it, too," Banks protested.

"Now you're doing exactly what I told you not to do,"

Mason said. "You're talking. My advice is, go see your sister. Talk with her, and remember she put up five thousand dollars in cash for bail."

"Where did she get that money?" Banks asked.

Mason smiled and said, "I'm not prepared to discuss the financial affairs of my client, and I am going to repeat once more to you that the best thing you can do is to keep your mouth shut until you've seen your sister, and see an attorney. My best guess is that you should go to see your sister now. Do you know where to find her?"

"I think I do."

"Do you know where she is *now?*"

"I can find her all right."

"Then you'd better go see her," Mason said. "You're out on bail. You're free to leave. That winds up my responsibility as far as you are concerned. I have places to go and things to do. Good luck."

Mason turned, walked out of the room, and took the elevator down to the entrance where Della Street was parked in the car.

"Well?" she asked.

"The plot thickens," Mason said. "Apparently everybody was betting on Dough Boy. There was a hot tip from somewhere.

"It now appears the amount of the embezzlement was only a little over a thousand dollars and the winnings on Rodney Banks' ticket would have been more than enough to have squared up everything, but Fremont claims the betting was done with funds that had been embezzled and therefore, since the money came from his till, he's entitled to the winnings."

"Can he do that?" Della Street asked. "Doesn't he have to do one or the other?"

"Technically," Mason said, "he's within his rights. The money was embezzled and it remained his money. If it was put out on a profitable investment, he's entitled to the profits."

"And can still prosecute for the embezzlement?"

"Embezzlement," Mason said, "is a crime, it doesn't give the embezzler title to the money. If he doesn't have title to the money, he isn't entitled to profits on the money."

"But how about the money our client bet on Dough Boy?"

"There's a question," Mason said. "A great deal depends on the embezzlement, how the money was embezzled and where it came from. Now, if Rodney gave his sister five hundred dollars and told her to bet it on Dough Boy, and that money was embezzled and Fremont can prove that it was embezzled from him, Fremont is entitled to all of the money that was won. But he's got to prove a lot of things. He has to prove the embezzlement, he has to prove the identity of the money, and he probably would have to prove that the sister was an accessory or at least had guilty knowledge. It's an unusual situation."

"Did Rodney act as if he knew his sister had bet on Dough Boy?"

"It's hard to tell," Mason said. "Rodney Banks is a chunky, broad-shouldered young man with quick, nervous speech and mannerisms—you just can't tell too much about the guy. He's typical of a certain brand of instability. You frequently find it in young men who have had mothers or sisters who have tried to protect them from the responsibilities of life."

"In other words, you don't like him and don't want any part of him?"

Mason grinned and said, "Let's put it this way. I'm not representing him. I represented his sister for the purpose of getting him out on bail. I've got him out on bail.

"And now, Miss Street, despite the early hour, since you have made a substantial winning on the horse races, we are going out to indulge in cocktails and an early dinner. We will forget dull care, crooked clients, penurious bosses, embezzlements and concentrate on rhythm, food, relaxation and enjoyment."

Chapter 6

It was still early when Perry Mason escorted Della Street to the door of her apartment house, said good night, then leisurely drove back to his own apartment.

The phone was ringing as he entered the door.

Since only Della Street and Paul Drake had the number of that phone, the lawyer hastened across the room to answer it.

"Hello," he said, "what is it?"

Paul Drake's voice came over the wire. "Your female client is in a dither. She wants you to come see her *right* away. She says it's terribly important, and she means *terribly* important."

"Well," Mason said. "I'm not chasing down there after office hours until I know what it's all about. I've discharged all my obligations to her. Did she tell you what was bothering her?"

"Some terrific emergency. She seemed all shaken up. Why not at least give her a ring," Drake said. "I think something important really has happened."

"Probably someone stuck her up and took her money away from her," Mason said. "Okay, I'll give her a ring."

Mason rang the Foley Motel, asked for Nancy Banks in 14.

The voice answering the phone said, "I'm sorry, but that number isn't answering right at the moment. I just had a couple of calls with no answer. I'm the manager."

"Perhaps I can try again in a few minutes."

The manager's voice said, with gentle but firm austerity, "May I ask who's calling, please?"

Mason hesitated a moment, then said, "If she should check in, tell her that her lawyer was calling her, will you please?".

"Her lawyer?"

"That's right."

"Well, why should she need—Oh, very well. Do you care to leave your name?"

"Mason."

"Not *Perry* Mason!"

"That's right.".

"Oh, I'm *so* sorry, Mr. Mason. I'll skip down there and leave a note on her door. She should be in any minute. I don't know *where* she is. I've had a couple of calls and she hasn't answered. I dislike ringing when a person isn't in. You know how it is. The walls are reasonably soundproof, but a ringing telephone *can* disturb the occupants of adjoining units."

Mason said, "I'll give you a ring a little later on. You can leave a note, if you will, just telling her that I've called, and will call again in ten or fifteen minutes."

The lawyer stretched out in an easy chair, lit a cigarette and was picking up the evening paper when the phone rang again.

Mason answered it and heard Drake's voice. "Perry, this girl is really in a state. She's excited as all hell and she says she has to see you at once, that you should get down there, that something terrible has happened."

"Get down where, Paul?"

"Down to the motel."

"She isn't there," Mason said. "The manager of the motel says she isn't answering the phone."

"She's there. That's where she phoned from," Drake said. "At least, that's where she *said* she was phoning from. I asked where she was and she said she simply had to see you, that she'd pay whatever it was worth if you could come down there right away, but that you must come there, she couldn't go to you. She said it was a great emergency."

"Oh, heck," Mason said, "that's what comes of getting tied up with feminine clients who get hysterical. . . . Okay, Paul, I'll take a run down there and if that girl isn't there I'll certainly make a charge that will teach her a lesson. . . . When are *you* going home?"

"Lord knows," Drake said. "I'm working on a rather difficult case. I've had a couple of men out and have been checking reports. What do you want to do about any future calls that come in?"

"Simply tell whoever is calling that I can't be reached until morning," Mason said. "But if this Nancy Banks telephones again, tell her I'm on my way down, and tell her that it had better be *really* important."

Mason sighed, adjusted his tie, and telephoned the apartment garage to have his car ready. He took the elevator to the garage and made time to the Foley Motel.

The vivid lights at the front of the motel blazoned, FOLEY MOTEL, and underneath, a relatively small sign, *No Vacancy*.

Mason hesitated a moment over whether to stop at the manager's office, then thought better of it and drove directly to Unit 14.

He parked his car, knocked on the door.

There was no answer, although lights were on in the unit.

Frowning, Mason tried the door. It opened readily.

On the floor just in front of the door was a note, "Miss Banks: Your lawyer called and said he would call back again in fifteen or twenty minutes."

Mason closed the door behind him, looked around the unit.

It was just as he had seen it last, a typical motel unit. A suitcase was on a stand. A feminine overnight bag was on the dressing table in front of the mirror.

Mason glanced at his watch, frowned his annoyance, seated himself and waited.

In the silence the lawyer became conscious of a spring-wound traveling clock on the bureau, ticking away the

47

minutes. He checked his time with that of the traveling clock, found that the traveling clock was five minutes slow, stretched, yawned, looked at his watch again and got up to leave.

Just as he was on the point of opening the outer door he paused to give the motel unit one more searching glance, then let his eyes come to rest on the closed door, apparently leading to the bathroom.

Mason crossed over to the closed door, knocked gently, received no answer and opened the door.

The body of Marvin Fremont was slumped grotesquely in the shower stall, the head over on one shoulder, the eyes staring vacantly, the jaw sagging. There was a small red stain, apparently from a bullet hole, in the front of his shirt.

Mason hesitated a moment, whipped out his handkerchief, polished his fingerprints off the doorknob to the bathroom, backed out of the bathroom into the room, pulled the door shut behind him and was halfway across the room when the outer door opened and Nancy Banks came hurrying into the room.

"Oh, Mr. Mason!" she exclaimed. "I'm *so* glad you came! Oh, this is such a relief! . . . Oh . . . Oh . . ." She put her hand to her throat. "Oh, thank you! Thank you so much!"

She came to the lawyer, took his hands in both of hers. Her hands were ice cold.

Mason said, "All right, quick. What's the story? Let's have it."

She said, "I have been calling you. I wanted you—"

"I called back and you didn't answer," Mason said.

"I wasn't here."

"That's obvious," Mason told her. "At least that's your story. Now, you'd better tell me *all* of it."

She said, "I went to my apartment. I . . . I wanted to put that money you left with me in a safe place."

"What was a safe place?"

"I wanted to hide it in my apartment, and I thought I'd

give some to a friend of mine for safekeeping. . . . I didn't want to have all of my eggs in one basket."

"Okay," Mason said, "let's get it all and get it fast. What happened? Why did you call me?"

She said, "Someone held me up."

"What do you mean, they held you up?"

"Just that. When I got out of my automobile in back of the apartment house, somebody pushed a gun at me and said in a low, gruff voice, 'Stick 'em up!' "

"Can you describe him?" Mason asked.

"He was—No, I can't."

"Did he have a mask on?"

"There was a handkerchief around his forehead, held in place by his hat and stretching down over his face. There were two holes in it for his eyes and that was all. All I could see was that white handkerchief and—"

"How was he built?" Mason asked.

"He was . . . he was broad-shouldered, stocky. I would say, from his figure and the way he moved, he was about . . . oh, about forty, or he *could* have been younger."

"I see," Mason said. "What happened?"

"He had me dead to rights. The money was in my bag. He just pushed that gun at me and . . . I started to scream and then he hit me and grabbed the bag and was gone."

"The whole amount?" Mason asked.

"The whole thing. All of it. Every cent of it, Mr. Mason."

The lawyer regarded her thoughtfully. "So you telephoned me?"

"Yes."

"Where did you phone from?"

"My apartment."

"You said you were here, didn't you? Isn't that the message you left with Paul Drake?"

"Yes, because I wanted you to meet me here."

"So you told Paul Drake you were phoning from here."

"Yes."

"Did you notify the police?"

"Heavens, no."

"Well," Mason said, his eyes on her face, "that's the thing you have to do. You're going to have to notify the police about the holdup. Why was it so important that you get hold of me and have me come *here*?"

Her eyes became round with surprise. "Why was it so important? Good heavens, Mr. Mason, a girl loses all her winnings in a holdup and you act as though it wasn't important. It's absolutely ruinous."

Mason nodded thoughtfully, said, "You'll have to notify the police."

"I can't, Mr. Mason. I simply can't."

"Why not?"

"Well, there are . . . certain reasons."

Mason said, "You've salvaged some of the money because I put up bail for your brother. You can get that back."

"Yes," she said, lowering her eyes.

"I still say we have to notify the police," Mason insisted. She shook her head vehemently.

"All right," Mason told her, "if that's the way you feel about it, there's nothing to be done except grin and bear it."

He moved over to the door, smiled at her and said, "You have to get accustomed to these things. After all, you're better off than you were a couple of days ago. You'll get the bail money back and you'll be ahead of the game."

"Mr. Mason, I . . . I'm disappointed in you."

"Why?"

"You're taking this so . . . so matter-of-factly."

Mason said, "A holdup is a new experience for you. This is the first time you've had someone point a gun at you and take any money. The police regard it as a matter of routine, just as you would if your employer asked you to bring a pencil and shorthand notebook and take a letter.

"Now, I'm not the police, but I see a great deal of crime, and I take things somewhat the same way.

"I don't like to argue with you. I suggest that you call the police. With the description you have of the individual, there's always the possibility that the police would recover the money."

"No, no, I can't stand that. I *don't* want the police."

"All right," Mason told her, "under those circumstances the only thing for me to do is to go home, the only thing for you to do is to go to bed, and—"

"But I'm afraid to stay here alone."

"What are you afraid of? You've lost your money. There's nothing else to be afraid of, is there?"

"No, I . . . I guess not."

"I can't stay here with you," Mason said. "You're a big girl now, you know . . . You said something about a friend you were going to leave the money with—a girl friend?"

"Yes."

"Why don't you go back to your apartment and get her to spend the night with you if you're nervous?"

"I—That's a good idea, Mr. Mason. I think I will. I'm glad you suggested it. I'll pack up right now."

"Okay," Mason told her.

She came across the room to give Mason her hand. It was still ice cold, and the lawyer could feel the nervous tremor running through it.

"All right, you do that," Mason said.

"Would you—Could you wait here while I pack up?"

"I'm sorry," Mason told her, "but I've had quite a day. You won't have any trouble now. Just put your things in the car and go back to your apartment."

"You—Well . . . if you could wait just a *few* minutes . . . "

Mason shook his head.

"I know," she said. "I understand. You're terribly busy and I guess you are pretty well bushed. . . . I guess you're

51

out of patience with me because I won't call the police. All right, thank you again, Mr. Mason. Thank you so much."

Mason smiled, patted her on the back and walked out the door.

He had reached a point about halfway to the office of the manager when he heard a door open behind him, the sound of running steps, and the young woman's voice. "Mr. Mason, please—oh, *please!*"

The lawyer turned.

She ran up and literally flung herself on him, hugging him to her in an ecstasy of terror. "Mr. Mason, please . . . please!"

"What is it this time?" he asked.

"Something terrible—something awful! You must . . . hush! We can't talk it over here, someone will hear us . . . . Please come."

"Something new?" the lawyer asked.

"Something terrible."

"What?" he asked.

"A . . ." She lowered her voice to a whisper. "A body."

"Where?"

"In the shower."

"You're sure?"

"Yes."

"Man or woman?"

"Man."

"Is he dead?"

"I don't know. I . . . I'm afraid he is. He looks dead."

Mason turned, put his arm around the trembling young woman, said, "All right, take it easy now. You're going to have to pull yourself together. You had no idea the body was there?"

"Heavens, no!"

"How did you find it?"

"I was going to get my things together and I . . . I went

to the bathroom and he was there, all crumpled up in the shower."

"All right," Mason said, "now we *have* to notify the police."

"Do we have to?"

"Yes."

"Can I leave and let you—"

"You can do nothing of the sort," Mason said. "That would be the worst thing you could do. You have to stay now and face the music."

"I . . . I—"

"You're afraid of the police, aren't you?" Mason asked.

"Yes, terribly."

"You shouldn't be," Mason said. "They'll give you your best protection if you're innocent . . . and you *are* innocent, aren't you?"

"Yes, of course."

"You knew nothing about the body being there?"

"No."

Mason held the door of the unit open for her.

"Oh, I hate to go in," she said. "I—"

"Sure you do," Mason told her, "but you've got to face the music."

He gently eased her into the unit, then kicked the door shut.

"Now then," he said, "suppose you quit lying."

"What do you mean?"

"You knew the body was there."

She looked at him with wide-eyed indignation. "Why, Mr. Mason. I—Why, how can you accuse me of anything like that?"

The lawyer's eyes regarded her steadily.

After a moment her eyes faltered.

"The reason you wanted me to come down here," Mason said, "the reason you were so anxious to have me meet you in this motel room, was that you knew the body was here. Either you killed him or you had discovered the body.

"You didn't want to tell me about it. You wanted me to be the one to discover it. You thought I'd discover it and call the police. You were going to enter the unit with this story about a holdup and—"

"That story about the holdup was true, Mr. Mason."

"I don't believe it," Mason said. "It was an alibi you concocted, and rather a crude alibi, to account for your absence and your excitement. The reason you called me was because you knew the body was there. I tricked you. Instead of discovering the body and telephoning the police, I pretended that I knew nothing about the body being there."

"You . . . you'd seen it?"

"Of course."

"But you didn't let on. You—"

"I was testing you," Mason said. "I wanted to see if you'd break down and tell me, or if you'd try to pull this phony stunt of pretending that you didn't know it was there and had gone to the bathroom and found it, and then dashed out to overtake me before I left."

She suddenly flung herself in his arms and started sobbing.

"That's what happened?" Mason asked.

"Yes," she said in a low voice. "That's why I telephoned you. I . . . I had found the body."

"How did you find it?"

"How would you expect? I had been out and when I came home I had to go to the bathroom and . . . there he was."

"All right," Mason told her, "we've got to notify the police. Now, the main thing is for you to tell me the truth *now*."

"I've told it to you."

"All of it?"

"All of it."

"What about the holdup?"

"It was true. It happened."

Mason said, "Do you want to wait in the unit while I call the police?"

"Heavens, no!"

"We'd better not call through the manager's office," Mason said. "That would make even more trouble. There's a telephone booth down by the swimming pool. We'll use that. You have a key to this place?"

"Yes."

"Lock it," Mason said. "Come with me."

They closed and locked the outer door. Mason escorted her to the end of the swimming pool, then to the telephone booth. He dropped in a dime, dialed operator, said, "Police Headquarters, please. This is an emergency."

When Headquarters answered, he said, "Perry Mason talking. May I speak with the Homicide Department, please?"

A moment later Lt. Tragg's voice came on the line. "Well, well, Perry. What is it this time? Not another murder, I hope."

"Apparently it is," Mason said.

"Where are you now?"

Mason told him.

"Where's the body?"

"In one of the motel units here."

"Are you alone?"

"No, I have my client with me."

"She's the occupant of the unit?"

"Yes."

"Who discovered the body?"

"I did."

"Why did she kill him, self-defense?"

"She says she didn't kill him."

"You've done nothing about moving or touching the body?"

"That's right. The body's in the shower; that is, half in and half out of the shower stall."

"And your client knows nothing about it."

"That's right."

"Then why did she call you?"

"It was on another matter."

"Keep out of the place, don't touch anything, don't leave any more fingerprints, don't leave and don't let your client try to leave," Lt. Tragg said. "We'll be out."

Chapter 7

Lt. Tragg of Homicide emerged from the motel unit to stand by Mason's car where Mason sat with Nancy Banks.

"All right, young woman," he said. "You had that motel room. Why did you rent it?"

"I . . . I wanted to have a place where I could talk with Mr. Mason privately."

"About what?"

"About some business affairs that don't need to enter into the picture."

"Now, let's come down to earth," Tragg said. "A murder was committed in that motel unit. Where were you when the crime was committed?"

"I don't know. I don't know what time the crime was committed."

"When did you discover the body?"

"When I came back."

"Back from where?"

"Back from my apartment."

"Where is your apartment?"

She told him.

"What were you doing there?"

"I went there to . . . to attend to some things that— Well, I had some money I wanted to dispose of."

"What do you mean, dispose of?"

"I wanted to put it where someone wouldn't find it."

"What someone?"

"No particular someone."

"All this sounds very interesting," Tragg said. "I'd like to know a little more about that."

Mason said, "Now, just a moment, Lieutenant. Let's have it understood that this questioning is not going to be done in what we might call an accusing manner."

Tragg said, "Then we'd better have an understanding that the answers aren't going to be made in what you might call an evasive manner."

Mason said, "The story is not a simple one, Lieutenant. Miss Banks has a brother. The brother had been arrested for embezzlement and—"

"Now, wait a minute," Tragg interrupted. "When I want a statement from you, Mason, I'll ask for it. Right now I want a statement from your client. I want some very definite answers to some very direct questions. I know what I'm driving at, and you may or may not know, but I don't want some smooth lawyer gumming up the works and tipping his client off to the answers she's supposed to make."

Mason turned to his client. "Go ahead, Nancy," he said. "Tell him. The very worst thing you can do right now is to let Lieutenant Tragg act under any misapprehension. He's a square shooter despite the fact that he's a hammer-and-tongs interrogator."

"That's better," Tragg said. "Now, Miss Banks, do you know this dead man?"

"Yes."

"Who is he?"

"He's Marvin Fremont."

"Do you have any connection with him?"

"I— My brother works for him."

"What does Fremont do? What's his line?"

"He's an investor. He deals in antiques and curios, and he buys and sells real estate on the side."

"You have trouble with him?"

"My brother did."

"What kind of trouble?"

"He accused my brother of embezzlement."

"Any other trouble?"

"My brother went to a horse race and bet on a winning horse and— Well, Mr. Fremont wanted the money."

"What money?"

"The money that was won."

"Did he get it?"

"Apparently so. He had my brother arrested and thrown in jail, and they took the winning ticket away from him, and Mr. Fremont filed a lawsuit and was going to get the money."

Mason started to say something, then, at a glance from Tragg, checked himself.

"Now, you retained Perry Mason. What for, to help your brother?"

"Yes."

"Anything else?"

"I wanted to get bail, that is, to put up bail so my brother could get out."

"What kind of bail?"

"Cash."

"Who furnished the cash?"

"I did."

"Where'd you get it?"

"I bet on a winning horse."

"What horse?"

"Dough Boy."

"What odds?"

"I put five hundred dollars on him to win and got . . . well, a rather nice stake, some fourteen thousand dollars."

"What did you do with it?"

"I didn't collect personally. I gave the tickets to Mr. Mason and he collected."

"What did Mr. Mason do with the money?"

"He turned it over to me."

"Then what?"

"Then I asked him to put up bail for my brother in the amount of five thousand dollars and gave Mr. Mason five thousand dollars for that purpose, and paid him his fee."

"And he put up the bail?"

"Yes."

"And what happened to the balance of the money?"

"I had it."

"Where is it now?"

"I lost it."

"How?"

"I was held up."

"When?"

"When I went to my apartment to conceal the money and to . . . well, to fix it so I wouldn't have all of my eggs in one basket. I wanted to have someone take part of it."

"Who?"

"Mrs. Lawton."

"What's her first name?"

"Lorraine."

"Where does she live?"

"She has the apartment across the hall from mine."

"What does she do?"

"She doesn't have to work. That is, she isn't dependent on work. She . . . she's been married."

"Alimony?"

"I believe so, yes."

"You know, don't you?"

"Well, mostly alimony."

"Other contributions?"

"She manages a trout farm, part of the time."

"What trout farm?"

"Osgood's Trout Farm. There's a pool there. You rent an outfit and catch trout and they charge you for each trout you catch. She works there sometimes. She knows Mr. Osgood, the owner."

"Did you give her part of the money?"

"No."

"Why not?"

"I was held up before I could see her."

"What happened to the money?"

60

"The man who held me up took it."

"What's the name of the apartment house?"

"The Lockhard."

"Where?"

"Lockhard Avenue."

"What's the number of your apartment?"

"513."

"Who was the man who held you up?"

"I don't know."

"Describe him."

"He was rather sort. I think he was about forty. He had a mask that had been made by putting a handkerchief around his forehead, holding it in place with a hat and letting the handkerchief hang down over his face. There were two holes cut for his eyes. All I could see was the hat, the handkerchief and the eyes. I . . . I knew he smoked because I could smell tobacco."

"Did he have a gun?"

"Yes."

"Did he get the money?"

"Yes, of course. He took it from me."

"What makes you think he was about forty?"

"His manner, the way he moved, his figure, his voice."

"Where did this holdup take place?"

"Where I park my car, the parking lot near the apartment house where most of the people in the apartment house park their automobiles."

"Do you leave yours there?"

"Yes."

"Regularly?"

"Yes."

"Parking attendant?"

"No. It isn't really a formal parking lot. It's a vacant lot that's owned by the man who owns the apartment house, and he lets the tenants park there."

"Any sign to that effect?"

"Yes. There's a sign that says parking is for tenants of the apartment house only, but out there very few other people would want to park—That is, it's the only large apartment house in the neighborhood."

"Think you'd know this man if you saw him again?"

"If I saw him wearing the mask, I *might*—I doubt it. I never saw his face at all."

"How tall?"

"Rather short. He was only an inch or two taller than I am."

"How heavy?"

"Well, he was reasonably heavy, sort of . . . well, about fortyish heavy."

"Chunky?"

"I suppose you'd call him that."

Tragg reached in his pocket, whipped out a handkerchief in which two eye holes had been cut. He placed it on his forehead, pulled his hat down to hold the handkerchief in place at just the right elevation so his eyes showed through the holes in the handkerchief. "Like this?" he asked.

Nancy Banks gave a little scream.

"Remind you of something?"

"You look—you look *exactly* like the man."

"Well, I didn't hold you up," Tragg said. "For your information, I got that handkerchief from the dead man's pocket."

"Oh!" she said. "Oh . . . !"

Tragg listened to the tone of the exclamation.

"Surprise you?"

"Yes."

"You didn't think he was the one?"

"I—It never occurred to me."

"But he could have been?"

"Yes."

"All right. Now, you left your apartment house and came back here to this motel?"

"Yes."

"And this dead man was there?"

62

"Well, it . . . it wasn't quite that simple. I didn't find him until— "

"He was there?"

"I suppose so, yes."

"When did you find him?"

"I . . . I don't know the exact time, but I called Paul Drake, the detective, before I had found him. I was told I could reach Mr. Mason at night through the Drake Detective Agency."

"So you called?"

"Yes."

"From here?"

"No, from a phone booth out along the road."

"Any answer?"

"Yes, I talked with Mr. Drake personally. I told him I had to see Mr. Mason at once on a matter of great importance."

"By that matter of great importance you meant the holdup?"

"Yes."

"But you didn't get Mason right away?"

"No."

"How long?"

"It seemed hours."

"Was it as much as an hour?"

"All of that."

"Two hours?"

"I don't know. I don't think so."

"Where were you all of that time?"

"At the phone booth."

"Where was that phone booth?"

"At a filling station."

"Where?"

"I can't tell you the address."

"Was the filling station open or closed?"

"Closed."

"Could you find that filling station?"

"I think so. It was on the road between here and my apartment. I guess I could probably find it again."

"Then what happened?"

"After a while Mr. Mason called Mr. Drake's office and got my message, and then I called Mr. Drake and he said Mr. Mason was on his way out."

"So Mr. Mason came out?"

"Yes."

"And you told him about the body?"

She hesitated.

"Well?" Tragg asked.

"No," she said, "not right away."

"Why not right away?"

"After I found the body, I went out and waited where I could watch. I wanted Mr. Mason to find the body. I wanted to pretend to him that—Oh, I don't know, I wanted to . . . to give myself an alibi, I guess . . . "

"Thought you'd be suspected?"

"I . . . I just didn't know. I got in a panic."

"Why?"

"Put yourself in her shoes, Lieutenant," Mason said. "You're in a motel, you find a body and—"

"I'm putting myself in her shoes," Tragg said. "I'm also going to ask *you* some questions a little later. Your skirts may not be as clean as you think they are. There may be angles about this case you know nothing about. Now then, Miss Banks, what made you think you'd be suspected?"

"Well, because the dead man and I, we didn't like each other."

"Over what?"

"Over the way he treated Rodney."

"Rodney's your brother?"

"Yes."

"Fremont had your brother arrested for embezzlement?"

"Yes."

"You knew Fremont?"

"Yes, of course."

"And had talked with him many times?"

"Yes."

"Had you ever worked for him?"

"Yes."

"Did you quit or were you fired?"

"I quit."

"Why?"

"Personal reasons."

Tragg said, "You discovered Fremont's body in your shower bath. You went into a panic and telephoned Mason. Then you went out and waited for Mason to come. What else did you do during that time?"

"I— Why, I just waited, that's all . . . Only I hadn't discovered the body when I first telephoned. You're getting me all mixed up. I phoned at first about the holdup. That is what I wanted to see Mr. Mason about. And then when I knew he was going to go to the motel to see me, I went there to meet him. That was when I discovered the body and went out to a place where I could watch for Mr. Mason to come."

"Just a minute, stay right there," Tragg said. "Both of you stop there."

He walked back into the motel unit, came out carrying a piece of torn cardboard dangling from a string. The string was looped around his forefinger.

"Ever see this before? Know what it is? What it was used for?" he asked Nancy Banks.

She shook her head. "Why . . . I . . . I . . ."

Her voice trailed away into silence. Mason regarded her sharply. Her face was drawn and white, the eyes wide with panic.

"I think we've had enough questioning, Tragg," he said.

Lt. Tragg grinned. "The answer to that question is going to hurt, eh?"

"I didn't say that."

"I said it, and your client's face shows it," Tragg said. "You know what this is, Miss Banks?"

She shook her head.

"Don't answer, Nancy," Mason said. "It's quite evident that the shock of finding the body in your room in the motel, the strain that you've been under the past few hours, has been too much for you. You're ready to collapse. I'm going to have to insist that there be no more questions and answers."

Tragg grinned and said, "All right, Perry. I haven't been under that much of a strain for the last few hours and I can answer the question. I'll tell you what it is. It's part of a dry ice container.

"For your information, an attempt was made to alter the time of the killing. Whoever killed Marvin Fremont wanted to confuse the issue as to the time of death and so packed the body in dry ice. Then, after the body had become chilled with the dry ice, an attempt was made to take all the containers, remove them, and let the police think the murder had been committed a few hours earlier than had actually been the case.

"However, the murderer or *murderess,* overlooked this torn part of one container of dry ice which we found *under* the body. It had evidently been torn loose from the container when the dry ice package was moved; however, there's enough printing left on the dry ice container to show part of the label, and when we find the other part of the original container, we can fit the piece into place.

"As a matter of fact, we probably would have become suspicious anyway because the tile floor of that shower bath was positively cold to the touch—I mean, ice cold—but this fragment from a container of dry ice clinches things.

"Now I'll tell both of you what that means and you can be thinking it over, Miss Nancy Banks. It means that that murder was deliberately planned. It means that it was a premeditated crime, carried out with fiendish ingenuity.

"And this one container, which your client has said by a shake of her head she knows nothing about, Mr. Mason, is a dead giveaway as to what happened. Now then, if we find your client's fingerprints on this container which she has said she knows nothing about—"

"Wait a minute," Mason said, "just so you don't put words in her mouth or distort the situation, she didn't say anything of the sort."

"She shook her head," Tragg said.

"She didn't shake her head in response to the question that she knew nothing about it. You asked her if she knew what it was and what it had been used for, and she shook her head."

"Well, she can either shake it or nod it right now," Tragg said. "I'll put the question to you, Miss Banks. Have you ever seen this container before? Have you ever touched it?"

"I told you she's not answering any more questions," Mason said.

"She could either shake her head or nod her head. That's not going to take too much strength," Tragg said.

Mason put his arm around Nancy's shoulders. "Sit back, Nancy," he said. "Don't shake your head, don't nod it, don't try to answer questions, don't let yourself get worked up. This is regular routine police technique, taking a young woman at a time when she is emotionally upset and trying to force her to incriminate herself. Now, just take it easy and don't answer questions. Don't shake your head, don't nod your head, don't even flicker an eyelash. When you get in possession of your faculties and become more composed, we'll give Lieutenant Tragg an interview and answer all the questions he wants. Until then we're not saying another word."

Tragg grinned and said, "You're waiting until you see if one of her fingerprints is found on the container. Then you'll know which way the cat is going to jump.

"All right, now I'll tell you something, Mr. Perry Mason. As far as I'm concerned you won't get an answer to that question about the fingerprints until after the case gets to court. Then if you want to put your client on the witness stand to make a denial, you'll be wondering just what hole card the prosecutor has, whether it's a deuce or an ace.

"And since you don't want your client to answer any more questions, since you feel that she's emotionally disturbed and that any further attempt to interrogate her is an indication of police brutality, I'll advise you that there is no longer any necessity for your client to remain here. You can take her to her apartment or to a hotel or any place you want.

"The only thing I request is that she be available for further questioning tomorrow, and we wouldn't want her to do anything which would make her unavailable because that would be evidence of flight, and you wouldn't want that, Mr. Mason."

Tragg smiled benevolently at both of them, turned on his heel and walked back into the motel.

Chapter 8

Mason turned to Nancy Banks.

"Please, Mr. Mason," she said, "*please* get me away from here. Get me where they can't find me for a while."

Mason started the car, drove out of the motel to the main road and began driving aimlessly in a stream of traffic.

"Feel like talking, Nancy?" he asked.

"No."

"I'm afraid you're going to have to talk. Before the police interrogate you again, I'm going to have a complete understanding with you.

"Now, do you understand what will happen if you lie to me? I'll be making the wrong moves. Instead of getting you out of trouble I'll be leading you into trouble. They've baited a trap and I want to know just how serious it is."

"It couldn't be any more serious," she said, and started to cry.

"Wait a minute, wait a minute," Mason told her. "Save the tears until later. You can't afford to relax and start crying now. You're wound up like a clock and you've got to remain that way until you tell me the truth. What about the dry ice?"

"I don't know anything about it."

"You're lying," Mason said.

She said, "You don't trust me. Nobody trusts me any more. I might just as well lie my head off if that's the way everybody's going to act about things."

Mason said patiently, "I know you've been through a lot, Nancy, but you're playing some sort of a game with me and you're trying to play a game with the police. You can't get away with it.

"I think you know something about that dry ice. I'll tell you what *I* think. I think that you're trying to protect your brother. I think you feel your brother killed Marvin Fremont and you're trying to cover up for him. I think you're trying to make it appear that Fremont had been dead for a longer time than was the case. I think you would like to have it appear that he was killed while your brother was in jail. That would give your brother a perfect alibi."

"What in the world makes you think that?" she asked.

"Because," Mason said, "when you met me at the cabin, your hands were cold as ice. They couldn't have been any more chilled if you had been handling dry ice."

"Why, Mr. Mason, you're absolutely crazy—Why, I never heard anything like that! The idea of you making any such accusation. Don't you know that when a woman gets terribly nervous and upset and frightened her hands and feet get cold? Good Lord, if you think my hands were cold, you should have felt my feet."

Mason said, "Nancy, I'm not going to waste time with you because I don't have it to waste. I'm going to tell you that there's something very, very wrong with your story and with the evidence, and I'm going to tell you that you are underestimating the police."

"How am I underestimating them?"

"They're a lot smarter than you think, and I know Tragg well enough to know he's baiting a trap for us."

"What sort of a trap?"

"He thinks we're going to do something, something that will play right into his hands. . . . Now, do you know anything about dry ice?"

"A little, a very little. Why?"

"That piece of cardboard that he had," Mason said. "I couldn't see all of the printing that was on it, but I could see a part of the letter C and the full letter E. Now, Tragg tells me that came from a package of dry ice and I'm not inclined to question his word. I don't think he would lie to us."

She said with a sudden burst of temper, "That damned dry ice!"

"What's the matter with it?" Mason asked. "What is there about it that knocks you for a loop? The minute Tragg mentioned dry ice you just about collapsed."

"All right," she said wearily, "I guess I'm going to have to tell you the truth."

"It might be better," Mason said. "You did handle the dry ice, didn't you?"

She hesitated a moment, then said, "Yes."

"Why did you put it there?" Mason asked.

"I didn't put it there."

"But you knew about it?"

"Yes."

"Did you touch it?"

"Mr. Mason," she said, "when I first found the body, it was just packed in dry ice and— Well, there were ten containers of dry ice all around the body; on the clothes, inside the coat, under the legs."

"What did you do?"

"I telephoned you and then I took the dry ice containers, put them in my car, drove frantically looking for a place to get rid of them and— Well, I found a culvert and threw them in there. Then I came back to the motel to wait for you, but by that time you had reached there and you were waiting."

"You're lying again," Mason said. "You didn't intend to tell me about finding the body. You intended to let me find it for myself."

"That's right," she said. "I'll be fair with you on that, Mr. Mason, but I'm telling you the truth about the dry ice."

"And what was so terribly incriminating about that?" Mason asked. "Why didn't you call the police and tell them about the body and let them find the dry ice?"

"Because that would have pointed directly to me."

"In what way?"

"I . . . I . . ."

"Go ahead," Mason said, "get it off your chest."

"It's a foolish remark I made, Mr. Mason. A group of us were talking about a week ago about murder, and someone mentioned how police determine body temperature to tell the time of a murder.

"I said a person could fool them by using dry ice and that I bet a person could commit the perfect crime by faking an alibi and packing the body in dry ice for a couple of hours so that when the police found the body they'd think the time of death was four or five hours earlier than had been the case."

"Who heard you say that?" Mason asked.

"The whole group. They kidded me about it."

"Who were in the group?"

"My brother, Lorraine, the manager of the Lockhard Apartments, her boy friend, and some friend of Lorraine's and another man named Halstead, who is the bookkeeper-manager of my brother's firm and some friend of his. We were all having a drink."

"Why did you happen to think of dry ice?"

"Because they use it at the trout farm and sometimes I go there with Lorraine and Rodney."

"He's friendly with Lorraine?"

"Yes."

"How friendly?"

"I haven't asked—I wouldn't know. I guess . . . quite friendly."

"Where does your brother stay?"

"He has a bachelor apartment in the Lockhard Apartments."

"And a key to Lorraine's apartment?"

"I wouldn't know. He's there a lot."

Mason sighed. "All right, Nancy, I've got news for you. The first thing that the police do in a case of this sort is start searching culverts. Experience has taught them that criminals use culverts as a favorite hiding place."

"Good heavens! Can't we . . . can't we go and get those containers out of the culvert?"

"We cannot," Mason said. "That would trap us both. In all probability Lieutenant Tragg has telephoned police headquarters and they're searching culverts right now. But you can gamble that when he turned us loose without any further questioning, it means he was prepared for us to go and trap ourselves. He'd given us the rope and he is now waiting to see us put that rope around our necks and hang ourselves.

"Bad as it is, we're not going to make it any worse.

"Come, Nancy, I'll take you back to your car and then you're going home. You're going to get your neighbor, Lorraine Lawton, to stay with you tonight. And I mean, *stay* with you. She's going to have to account for every minute of your time. She's going to have to be able to swear that you didn't leave your apartment from the time you entered it. I'm going to follow along behind you and see that no one tries to follow you. If I blink my lights rapidly, that means someone is trying to follow you. In that event, park your car and when I drive up get in with me and I'll take you to your apartment and stay with you until you can get Lorraine."

"Those dry ice containers, they—?"

"I'll put it to you frankly," Mason said. "If you make a single effort to get those dry ice containers, you'll be in so deep I'll never be able to get you out.

"Now then, what about the handkerchief? That was exactly the sort of handkerchief that was used in the holdup. Do you think Marvin Fremont engineered that holdup?"

"Mr. Mason, I don't know *what* to think."

"The person who held you up could have been Marvin Fremont?"

"Yes, it could have been."

"How long ago were you held up? Can you tell me about what time it was?"

"It must have been—I guess two or three hours. I don't have much sense about time. I have a watch but it never works. I almost always forget to take it off when I get in the shower."

"And how long had it been since you got to the cabin and discovered the body?"

She hesitated.

"Come on," Mason said, "I want the truth."

She said, "It was about—I guess about twenty minutes before you got there."

"In other words," Mason said, "it was after you knew I was on my way out that you took the dry ice containers and went out and threw them down the culvert?"

"Yes."

"Let's hope," Mason said, "that you didn't leave any fingerprints on that pasteboard."

"They can't get fingerprints from paper, can they?"

Mason said, "You seem to know a lot about police procedure and crime detection."

"I like to read the factual crime stories," she said. "I don't know why crime has always had a fascination for me. I read the true detective magazines."

"All right," Mason said, "I have information for you. It's hard to get fingerprints from paper under certain circumstances. It depends on the paper and the circumstances, but there's a new technique in use at the present time by which they develop fingerprints from the use of amino acids to get them from paper.

"Those amino acids have a delayed reaction with the surface of the paper and sometimes they can get fingerprints, and very fine fingerprints, even as much as several years after the fingers have touched the paper.

"The old method was mainly that of placing the paper in a container filled with iodine fumes and trying to develop latents that way. It wasn't always satisfactory and was

74

rather difficult. That's why the impression got around that it was pretty much of an impossibility to get fingerprints from paper. But with this new amino-acid technique it's possible to get fingerprints from paper."

"I didn't know that," she said.

Mason said, "If they find those dry ice containers and get your fingerprints on them, it would be deadly for you to try to explain what had happened, and it would be equally deadly for you to refuse to explain."

"You mean I'm in a bad fix?"

"I mean you're in a very bad fix," Mason said. "Now I'm going to tell you something else."

"What?"

"I think you're still lying to me. I think you're trying to protect someone, probably your brother."

"Mr. Mason, I am trying to tell you the truth."

"All right," Mason told her. "I'm not going to argue with you. I'm going to warn you that Lieutenant Tragg has baited a trap, that he expects you to underestimate the police and to walk right into the trap. I am going to warn you not to underestimate the police. They're deadly, they're clever, they're intelligent, and above all they're persistent.

"Now then, I'm going to drive you back to the motel. I'm going to put you in your car. You're going to start for your apartment. I'm going to follow along behind.

"I don't think that it occurred to Tragg that I would let you drive your car. I don't know. I think he thought I would try to take you directly to your apartment or perhaps hide you out somewhere.

"I'm going to take you back to your car and then I'm going to follow along behind you. I'll be probably a quarter of a mile behind you. If anybody passes me and gets between us, I'm going to follow along behind to see if he's trying to follow you and if he is, I'll pass him and blink lights several times.

"Now, you understand that, Nancy. If you see my lights blink, it will mean that you're being followed. As long as my lights are behind you and are steady, it means that there's no one coming along close enough to follow you. And if that happens it *may* mean that you're not under as much suspicion as I'm afraid may be the case.

"Now, if you are not under suspicion, it's because the police have uncovered some clue which points to somebody else. We can't tell about that until after some considerable time has elapsed. But I'm telling you this so that you won't lie awake and become a nervous wreck worrying about what may happen.

"If the police don't try to follow, it's a very reassuring sign, and if no one has tried to follow us by the time we get to your apartment, I think you can count on the fact that they've uncovered evidence pointing to someone else. So try to get a good night's sleep."

"Mr. Mason," she said, "I can't ever express my gratitude to you."

"The best thing you can do," Mason told her, "is to tell me the truth and follow my instructions.

"Now then, we're going back and get your car and you're going to head for your apartment. I'll see you safely there, then we'll get Lorraine and have things fixed so you can account for every minute of your time from now on."

"Very well," she said in a thin, worried voice.

"And," Mason said, "I have to phone Paul Drake and tell him about the murder. We're going to need his help."

Chapter 9

Mason let Nancy get a head-start, then swung in behind her and kept a fairly even distance, carefully watching in his rearview mirror to see if anyone was following.

He could see no one.

There was little traffic on this road, but Mason knew that within two miles when it entered a main freeway there would be plenty of traffic, and there was always the possibility that Tragg had an officer stationed there at the intersection ready to pick up the chase.

The taillights on his client's car swept around a curve. Mason held back, watching the rear. He began to speculate on whether Tragg's trap had to do with a shadow who would be waiting in a car at the freeway junction.

The lawyer speeded up, swept around the curve, and as the road straightened out, looked ahead for the taillights on Nancy Banks's car.

Not seeing them, the lawyer pushed hard on the foot throttle, watched the speedometer needle climb.

Half a mile from the intersection the lawyer picked up taillights ahead, saw the brake lights flash as the car came to a boulevard stop, then the lights were swallowed up in the rush of traffic on the freeway.

Mason himself was not so lucky. Having brought his car to a full stop at the boulevard intersection, it was nearly ten seconds before he got a break so he could get into the stream of traffic, which by that time was a mass of indistinguishable taillights.

Mason followed the freeway until he came to the turnoff

to Lockhard Avenue and followed the short street to the Lockhard Apartments.

He was unable to find a parking place closer than two blocks from the apartment house. He walked those two blocks, called Nancy Banks's apartment, got no answer. He found the name, Lorraine Lawton, on the name list and punched the button opposite Apartment 512, lifted the house phone receiver to his ear and waited.

After a moment he heard a very attractive feminine voice say, "This is Mrs. Lawton. Who is it, please?"

"I don't know whether you've heard of me or not," Mason said, "but I'm Perry Mason. I'm attorney for—"

"Oh, yes. Yes, indeed, Mr. Mason."

"Is Nancy Banks with you?"

"No, she isn't. Would you like to come up?"

"I expected Nancy Banks to have been here by the time I arrived. I'll wait down here a minute or two and come up with her."

"Oh, that'll be fine. I'd like to see you and . . . I have some things to tell you."

"Perhaps," Mason said, "I'd better come up before she gets here."

"Why not? She'll get in touch with me as soon as she does. My apartment is right across from hers."

"On my way," Mason told her.

"You turn to the left at the elevator, on the fifth floor. Mine's an inside apartment about four doors down."

"I'll be right up," Mason said.

The lawyer, frowning thoughtfully, took the elevator to the fifth floor, turned left and just as he reached the door of Apartment 512, it was opened and a young, attractive blue-eyed blonde smiled up at him.

"Mr. Mason?"

"Yes."

She gave him her hand. "I'm Lorraine Lawton. Come in, please."

"I expect Nancy will be here any moment," Mason said.

"In fact, I can't understand why she isn't here already. You haven't heard anything from her?"

Lorraine Lawton shook her head.

"I can't understand what happened to her," Mason said. "She should have been here several minutes ago."

"You're acting as attorney for Rodney, Mr. Mason?"

"Not for Rodney," Mason said. "I am at the moment acting as Nancy's attorney."

"What in the world does *she* need a lawyer for?"

"Well, for one thing," Mason said, "she retained me to get bail for Rodney."

"Bail for Rodney?"

"Yes."

"You mean that she's able to furnish bail? She's got a bond?"

Mason said, "I'd prefer she told you the details herself and she'll be here any minute, but that's generally the situation. I take it you're her close friend and also a friend of Rodney's?"

"Heavens, yes, Mr. Mason, she wouldn't keep any secrets from me—nothing. You can feel free to tell me anything. But I do hope you can get Rodney out. The idea of his being there in jail just— Well, it makes my flesh crawl."

"He's out," Mason said.

"He is? Why, he hasn't let me know about it," she said, pouting, and then added after a moment, "the stinker."

Mason said, "He'll probably be in touch with you. He probably had some things to do."

"That man Fremont," she said, "is in my opinion the most despicable man in the world. He's a crook and he's just going to ruin Rodney. I don't think a man should work for someone unless he can respect that individual and look up to him. I think it does something to a man's character when he has to put himself in a subservient position to some man who is . . . well, just a rotter."

"You know him?" Mason asked.

"Marvin Fremont? I'll say I know him."

Mason said, "I'd like to ask you a few things about Nancy. Does she know anything about dry ice? Do you know? Does she ever have occasion to use it?"

Lorraine laughed. "Good heavens, Mr. Mason, dry ice is right down her alley."

"What do you mean?"

"Well," she said, "I have a job of sorts. It's not a regular job. I can work at it as much as I want to and I get paid by the hour. It's helping manage the Osgood Trout Farm. And of course they keep dry ice out there."

"Could you tell me a little more about it?" Mason asked.

"Well," she said, "you've probably seen the sign. There's a turnoff on the highway. It says Osgood Trout Farm, One Quarter Mile. No Fishing License Needed. All the Trout You Want, a Full Catch Guaranteed.

"Well, people come in there and we give them the tackle and they go out to the pools and fish and we charge them so much a fish."

"They're able to catch all they want?" Mason asked.

"All they want," she said. "There are half a dozen pools on the place connected with a stream, and they're kept stocked with trout. Of course the trout are fed and actually are tame. When they see a person coming along the bank they think it means more feed and they come up looking for food. What the poor things don't realize is that sometimes this food is on a fishhook and then they're snaked out of the water and into the creel of the angler."

"And you run the place?"

"Well," she said, "it's a peculiar arrangement. There are three or four of us girls who are sort of props. We get paid by the hour when we work, mostly on Saturdays and Sundays."

"What do you mean, props?" Mason asked.

She laughed and said, "We put on bathing suits that really catch the eye and we go out there where we can be seen from the road right by the entrance to the farm. We have a fishing creel and a rod and we move around the place.

"Sometimes we have on a bathing suit but put a skirt and blouse over it and the customer doesn't know we have a bathing suit underneath. We put on boots and wade out in the water and pretend to get our skirts wet and give little screams and pull up our skirts and show a lot of leg and thigh and dress things up a bit.

"And then of course at times Mr. Osgood wants to leave the place and he will let us manage it while he's away. After all, there's nothing much to it. You simply check the customer in and then weigh his fish when he checks out. If they're below a certain length we charge him so much per fish. But if he catches a big one, we charge him by the ounce."

"We were talking about dry ice," Mason said.

"Oh, that's part of the business. We have a store of dry ice there in little pasteboard containers that are made up specially for us and we keep them in a storage vault, and when people want to take the trout home with them we sell them dry ice."

She laughed and said, "You'd be surprised, Mr. Mason, how many trout fishermen rely on us. We have people who are regular customers. They go out on a fishing trip way up into the mountains someplace and have poor luck. They come back and know the place, pull in there and believe me, they're all business. They don't see any sport about it and they don't want to do it for sport. They simply get out on the bank of the stream and haul in the fish one after another. Then they check in, buy dry ice and then drive on to their homes and tell their wives and friends about the wonderful trout fishing they had, and how skillful they are as anglers."

"You keep this dry ice locked up?" Mason asked.

"Oh, the whole place is locked at night and in the early morning, yes."

"But you have keys?"

"Yes."

"Does Nancy have keys?"

"I . . . I think she does."

"She's been working out there with you?"

"Yes, she has a cute figure in a bathing suit and she's really a wonderful actress when it comes to pretending to get her skirt wet wading. She'll have people just ogling at her from the banks, and cameras come out and she'll laugh and pose with her legs in the water up to the knees and her skirts up just as high as they can go without the photographer seeing there's a bathing suit underneath. Of course some of them get a glimpse of the suit but they laugh about it. She's been very popular."

"Mr. Mason, how about buying you a drink?"

"No thanks," Mason said, looking at his wristwatch. "I'm concerned about Nancy, and I am working."

"But why are you concerned about her?"

"She was supposed to meet me here."

"Well, she has a crazy sense of time, I'll tell you that about her, Mr. Mason. You make an appointment with her and she may be anywhere from fifteen minutes to half an hour late. I wouldn't worry about her not meeting you on time."

"This was a little different from an appointment," Mason said. "She was supposed to come here and I was following along behind."

"She might have had tire trouble."

"I didn't see anybody hung up along the road with tire trouble," Mason said. "Where is this Osgood Trout Farm?"

"Oh, it's down— Here, I have a map. I'll show you the place. This is a large-scale map and it tells all about how to get there and about the accommodations."

"There are accommodations there?"

"A snack bar," she said, "and beer and soft drinks, that's all. But there's a motel right near the place, within a mile and a half, and it's a very good motel. We recommend it. Here's the map."

"What's the name of it?" Mason asked, taking the printed folder. "The motel?"

"The Foley," she said.

"I see." The lawyer's face was impassive.

He walked over to the window, looked out into the light well, paused by the table and said, "I see you have a lot of true crime magazines here."

"Some that Nancy gave me after she finished with them. Nancy is a fiend on that stuff. I can either take it or leave it alone, but when she gives me the magazines I look through them and sometimes see something I like. Nancy is an omnivorous reader. She gives me all of her magazines and paperback books and I read them and then pass them on or get rid of them some way. I can't see spending money for all that crime stuff myself, but Nancy loves it.

"That's a peculiar thing your asking about the dry ice, because it was only a few nights ago that Nancy was talking about committing a perfect crime with dry ice. She said you could fool the police so that nobody could tell the time of a murder and a person could give himself a fake alibi that nobody could challenge."

Mason said, "Is there any printed matter on the cartons of dry ice that you have?"

"Yes, there are the words 'Dry Ice' and also we have a little ad from the trout farm printed on them."

Knuckles sounded on the door.

There was a peculiar rhythm to the knock, and suddenly Lorraine Lawton's face lit up.

"That's Rod now," she said, and ran to the door.

"Hi, Peaches," Rodney Banks said, sweeping her into his arms and kissing her, more as a routine gesture on his part than with any great amount of enthusiasm.

"Rod, you're out!"

"Sure. Sis bailed me out. Didn't you know?"

"How was I to know? And then you come barging in at this time of night. You didn't say anything, you stinker. You could at least have called."

"I had a little business to attend to— Well, what do you know? Perry Mason, the great lawyer!"

"Hello, Rodney," Mason said.

"Where's Sis?" Rodney asked.

"I don't know," Mason said. "She was to have met me here."

"Well, she'll show up anywhere from half an hour to an hour late. She has no sense of time."

"Rod, what happened?" Lorraine asked.

"That so-and-so had me picked up, claimed I was short in my accounts. Why, that old buzzard. I could flatten him into a grease spot. He can't prove there's a dime missing, and believe you me, once he gets into court to try and establish the cash structure of that business he's going to be in trouble—big trouble."

"But you're all right now, Rodney?"

"Oh, sure, I'm all right. I had a bad night down there in the hoosegow. . . . What a crummy joint that is. I can see why people keep on the straight and narrow path. They don't want to get mixed up in a joint like that."

"Why didn't you let me know as soon as you got out?"

"I told you I had some business to do. I had to collect some moxie, mazuma, lettuce, hay, scratch."

Rodney reached in his pocket, pulled out a billfold.

Mason, regarding the billfold thoughtfully, said, "You didn't have that with you when you were arrested, Rodney."

"Fortunately not," Rodney said. "I had it stashed away where I knew I could put my hand on it. I was afraid to take it down to the race track. I knew if I went down there with that mazuma I'd bet the whole thing. If I had a losing streak, I'd throw it all away. So I just took a definite amount of money and went down there. What makes me so damned mad is that after I'd picked a long shot the cops didn't let me cash my ticket.

"What can I do about that ticket, Mr. Mason? They say it's impounded in court."

"You'll have to get a lawyer," Mason said.

"I'm talking to one."

Mason smiled and shook his head. "I can't represent you, Rodney."

"Why not?"

"Because I'm representing your sister."

"Shucks, it's all right with Sis. Sis and I are one and the same."

"Not in this instance," Mason said. "You'd better have an attorney of your own."

Rodney said to Lorraine, "Well, come on, Lorraine, we're going out and do a little celebrating. . . . You going to come along for a nightcap, Mason, or are you going to wait for Sis?"

"I'll wait a little while," Mason said, "but I can't wait very long."

"Well, we'd better be going," Rodney said.

Mason said, "Just a minute. I have some news for you, both of you. Marvin Fremont is dead."

"What?" Rodney exclaimed.

Lorraine gave a little gasp and involuntarily recoiled.

Mason said, "You'll find this out either from the police or from the press and there's no reason why you shouldn't know it now. Nancy went to the Foley Motel. She rented a unit there. I don't know why. She had me meet her there to give her some money. I'd prefer that she herself told you how much and where the money came from.

"Now, it *may* be that she went to the motel because she was afraid someone was going to try to attach that money. I don't know.

"However, this much I do know. Marvin Fremont was found dead in her unit of the motel. He had been murdered. He had evidently been shot once, perhaps more. His body was lying sprawled in the shower."

"Well, *what* do you know," Rodney said.

"But what about the police?" Lorraine asked. "Do the police know?"

"The police know. They've been there. They've questioned Nancy and let her go. Nancy was to come directly here."

"Where were you?" Rodney asked.

"I was with her when the police came, and afterwards while they questioned her. I was supposed to be right behind her after they turned her loose. I was following along behind to make sure that the police weren't following. We rounded a turn in the road and when I got to the turn her lights had disappeared. There's a sort of S turn there and I thought she was on ahead. I put on speed and found taillights way ahead. At the time I thought they could be hers if she had really put on a burst of speed as soon as she rounded the corner."

"That first corner by the Foley Motel?" Lorraine asked. Mason nodded.

"Why, that's where you turn off to the Osgood Trout Farm. I'll bet she went to the farm and then you went on ahead and missed her. That would put her behind you. . . . That must be why you didn't see her any more."

"Well, what was Marvin Fremont doing in that motel?" Rodney asked. "And what was he doing in Sis's room?"

Mason said, "I was hoping *you* could tell *me*."

Rodney shook his head. "It's all news to me," he said. "What did the police say about it?"

"They seemed to have an idea that Nancy might have done it."

"That's a laugh," Rodney said. "Nancy wouldn't even slap a fly on the wrist."

Lorraine said, "Nancy seems to have been doing things in a mysterious way lately, Rod. . . . Why did she go to the motel in the first place?"

"So Mason could bring her some money to bail me out with," Rodney said.

"And how did Marvin Fremont know where she was?"

"Now, that's a question," Rodney said.

There was a moment of silence, then suddenly Rodney Banks flared. "By God, if Marvin Fremont was making any passes at Sis—if he had an idea he was going to parlay that situation with me into—Why, the sonofabitch!"

"Hush, Rod. He's dead."

"I don't give a damn whether he's dead or not. He was a sonofabitch alive and he's a sonofabitch dead."

"Rodney, don't talk like that. Don't talk about the dead that way."

"I'll talk about the dead any way I damned please," Rodney said. "Well, what do you know! Somebody finally gave old Fremont what he had coming to him. . . . Just where *is* Sis? You don't suppose the police picked her up?"

"I don't know," Mason said. "The police questioned her and turned her loose. Told her not to leave town, and to hold herself available for further questioning if necessary. If she went to the trout farm, she could have been picked up all right."

"Where do you fit into the picture?" Rodney asked. "You're representing her in the murder case?"

"She hasn't been charged with murder yet. I was representing her in this other matter."

"The bail business?"

"Yes."

"I see," Rodney said. "Where did she get the money?"

"I think you'll have to talk with your sister about that. She should be here any minute."

Rodney hesitated, looked at his watch, said, "Well, shucks. Sis can take care of herself. I know how she must feel, but Lorry and I are going out and look the town over and I don't think Nancy would be too happy tagging along . . . Look, honey, why don't you put the spring lock on, let Mr. Mason wait here for Nancy, and we'll go on out."

"I'm worried about her," Lorraine said.

"What is there to worry about? She can take care of herself. She's a good driver. She's been all over the city times without number. She used to drive to work every morning and make better time than I could. If the police are questioning her some more, Mason, here, can take over. . . . Tell me, Mr. Mason, Marvin Fremont got a court order or an attachment of some sort and picked up the ticket I had on Dough Boy to win. Now he's dead. What effect's that going to have on the litigation?"

"The cause of action that he had probably did not survive," Mason said, "but the administrator of his estate will be given an opportunity to be substituted as party plaintiff."

"You mean the money will be tied up?"

"For a while, yes."

"The hell with that stuff," Banks said. "I should be able to make the old buzzard pay for that."

"You can try to collect damages from his estate, but there again the cause of action would hardly survive."

"You lawyers and your surviving of actions," Banks said. "Come on, let's go, Lorry."

Lorraine Lawton said, "Would you mind waiting here, Mr. Mason? Or, you could wait across in Nancy's apartment. I have a key. We could let you wait there. You could leave the door open."

Mason looked at his watch, said, "I feel that under the circumstances there's not very much I can do here. I think I'll leave now and keep in touch with the Drake Detective Agency. If either of you hear anything about Nancy or want to get in touch with me, please call the Drake Detective Agency and leave a message. They're open twenty-four hours a day and I can get messages there."

"Okay, she'll get in touch with you," Rodney said. "Come on, Lorry. We're going out and trip the light fantastic. . . . Nice to have seen you again, Mason."

Chapter 10

From a phone booth Perry Mason called the office of Paul Drake.

When he had the detective on the line, Mason said, "Just checking in, Paul, to see if there's anything new. If there isn't, I'm going home and call it a day. I've lost my client. You might put an ear to the ground."

"What do you mean you've lost her?"

"She was to show up at the apartment of a friend," Mason said, "and she didn't make it."

"Police?"

"The police had turned her loose."

"Car accident?"

"I don't think so. She may have led with her chin. You'd better put an ear to the ground."

"Okay," Drake promised. "Will do. In the meantime I have another development waiting here that I think you'd better look into."

"What?"

"His name," Drake said, "is Larsen E. Halstead. He's the bookkeeper-manager of Fremont's business. He has a story."

"Will it keep?"

"It'll keep," Drake said, "but we can't keep it. The police have to know about it. I'm holding the guy here temporarily because I thought you might like to hear the story before the police do and thought it might be good public relations for you to telephone the police that—"

"Where is he?"

"My office."

"Can you hold him until I get there?"

"I think so. I've held him fifteen minutes already."

"I'm on my way," Mason said. "Do the best you can, and see if you can find out what's happened to Nancy Banks. Check with any police connections you may have."

Mason jumped in his car, drove rapidly to the parking lot adjoining his office building, left the car in the stall he rented by the month, and took the elevator to Paul Drake's office.

The telephone operator looked up as Mason opened the door, flashed him a smile, then motioned down the corridor toward Drake's office.

She was at the moment talking on the telephone.

Mason interpreted the sign language, opened the locked gate, went on down the corridor to Drake's rather small office.

A somewhat stooped man in his early fifties was sitting in a chair, his steel-rimmed glasses down on his nose so that he could, by raising his eyes, peer over them.

The man's hair was turning gray, his eyebrows were bushy and gray, his eyes were a pale blue, steady and appraising. He was slightly stooped, quiet, but not meek. His face had character.

Paul Drake performed the introductions. "This is Mr. Mason, Halstead," he said, and then to Perry Mason, "Larsen Halstead is the manager of Fremont's business. He has a story."

"How did you get in touch with him?" Mason asked.

Drake answered evasively, "It's a long story, Perry, but I thought you'd be interested in what Halstead has told me about the nature of Fremont's business. Suppose you tell Mr. Mason just as you told it to me, Halstead," Drake said, turning to the figure in the chair. "It might be a good plan to run over it once more."

Halstead cleared his throat and said, "I'm not certain of

my position in the matter. I don't like to make charges and– "

"That's all right," Drake said hastily. "Whatever you're saying is completely confidential."

"I'm afraid," Halstead said, "that Fremont is a crook. And I shouldn't say that about my employer, but I'm afraid I can't continue to work for him any longer. The man's methods are repulsive.

"You know he had Rodney Banks arrested for embezzlement. I think Rodney *may* have been a few dollars short, but Fremont really engineered the whole deal. He gave Rodney collections to make in cash over the weekends, knowing Rodney liked to go to the track and bet on the horses every weekend."

Mason exchanged glances with Paul Drake. "Why would he want to make an embezzler out of an employee?"

"On account of the sister, Miss Nancy. I'm here because of her. I understand she employed Mr. Drake. I gathered there was a connection. . . . Mr. Drake has refused to comment . . . but, of course, I can see you gentlemen are interested and that she is no stranger to you.

"Nancy worked for Fremont for a while. He couldn't keep his hands off of her. She slapped his face and walked out. He's been trying ever since to get some sort of a hold on her.

"Rodney kept on working for Fremont after his sister quit. He threatened to punch Fremont's face in if he ever made another pass at Nancy.

"Fremont laughed it off.

"Something should be done to help Rodney now. His arrest was only to enable Fremont to get Nancy where he wanted her.

"Fremont is a crook."

"In what way?" Mason asked.

"He's a fence."

"How do you know?"

"I stumbled on it somewhat accidentally. Fremont buys

and sells antiques, dabbles in speculative investments mostly related to real estate and has a rather sketchy sort of business that I never fully understood.

"One thing is certain. He doesn't cater generally to the public. He has the most sloppy place you can imagine; things are piled all over the place in confusion. The only thing that is modern about it is the safe in the office and his books. He keeps an elaborate set of books, and I've now come to the conclusion they don't mean anything."

"Why not?" Mason asked.

"His activities, his main activities, don't appear on the books. His other activities are accompanied with elaborate accountings."

"What are his main activities?"

"The man is a fence."

"What do you mean?"

"He buys up antique jewelry, the old settings that have, for instance, garnets or perhaps imitation rubies."

"Go ahead," Mason said.

"He'll have them around the shop for a while and then the gold setting which had contained a garnet will blossom into something else. The garnet will disappear and in its place will be a huge diamond."

"And then?" Mason asked.

"Then he'll sell the thing to one of the concerns that would take the good gems out of the antique gold settings, mount them in platinum and sell them and then sell off the antique settings."

"How did you get onto this?"

"I got onto it last week when I happened to recognize a piece that had been gold with several garnets. When I saw it last week two of the garnets had disappeared and in their places were sparkling diamonds, naturally making the whole piece very valuable indeed."

"I see," Mason said thoughtfully.

"Go on," Drake said. "Tell him the rest of it, Halstead."

"Well, of course, in order to carry on a business of that

sort, Mr. Mason, particularly one that doesn't appear on the books, it's necessary for a man to have huge sums of cash money."

"Fremont has such a sum?" Mason asked.

"He has it," Halstead said, "and I didn't find it until last week. I realized that my own activities in the matter might be subject to question because I am employed as bookkeeper, so I started making a secret inventory."

"Of what?"

"Of the cash."

"And it fluctuates?"

"I'll say it fluctuates. There was twenty thousand dollars in currency in a secret vault in the floor, and the amount fluctuated from day to day, getting as low as six thousand two hundred and seventy-five dollars one day, then going back to eighteen thousand dollars; then, early Friday morning, going down to a little over twelve thousand, then after Fremont came in it was up to over eighteen thousand again."

"And what happens to this money?"

"Undoubtedly some of it is used as payment to people who bring in stolen gems, but it could have been taken out by *any* person."

"Just what do you mean by that?" Mason asked.

"Rodney Banks is a good kid," Halstead said. "He's young and he has the arrogant chip-on-his-shoulder attitude that some young people have.

"Fremont is going to claim that Banks embezzled money from the liquid cash which we keep in the regular safe.

"Now, here's where I can help. I happen to know that one of the hundred-dollar bills that was in the liquid cash in the safe Thursday night turned up in the hidden cash in the concealed floor receptacle on Friday morning."

"How do you know?" Mason asked.

"Because I wrote down the number on the bill. I've been jotting down numbers on hundred-dollar bills ever since I found that secret hiding place in the floor."

Mason regarded the man thoughtfully. "You're going to have to go to the police with this," he said.

"I intend to go to the police. I want to keep my own skirts clean, but the point is that if cash was juggled from the liquid cash in the safe to this hidden hoard of money, then there's no way on earth of proving any embezzlement and— Well, the case against Rodney Banks blows sky high."

Mason looked at his watch, said, "Just a minute. I'll see if I can get the police."

Paul Drake raised his eyebrows. "Lieutenant Tragg?"

Mason nodded.

Drake picked up the phone, said to his switchboard operator, "Get Lieutenant Tragg at Homicide, if he hasn't gone home for the night."

"Homicide?" Halstead said, puzzled. "This is in the department which deals with cash shortages and embezzlements."

"Not now it isn't," Mason said. "It's in Homicide. Marvin Fremont was killed at the Foley Motel sometime earlier this evening."

"What!" Halstead exclaimed.

"Nancy Banks was there. The body was found in her room."

"That explains a lot," Halstead said thoughtfully. "Fremont told me he was satisfied Nancy had some of the embezzled money, and he was going to get it one way or another. He said she wouldn't dare go to the police no matter *what* happened."

Drake said, "Just a moment, Lieutenant Tragg. Perry Mason wants to talk with you," and handed the phone to Mason.

"Hello, Lieutenant," Mason said. "I didn't know whether you had left for the night."

"Don't you know we never go home?" Tragg said wryly.

Mason said, "I'm sending you a witness, if you want to wait there long enough to talk with him."

"What sort of a witness?"

"A man by the name of Larsen Halstead, who was employed by Fremont as bookkeeper-manager."

"We've been looking for him," Tragg said. "I located the place where he rooms and we've had a man staked out trying to get him. We want to talk with him."

"He's with me now and he'll be on his way up there by taxicab," Mason said.

"He's with you now?"

"Yes."

"Don't let him go by taxicab," Tragg said. "Don't let him out of your sight. We'll have a radio car call within a matter of minutes."

"I'm in Paul Drake's office," Mason said.

"I gathered as much," Tragg said, "because Drake put in the call and I suppose you've got this fellow all primed to tell exactly the kind of a story you want the police to believe."

"It's an interesting story," Mason said, "and we don't give a damn whether the police believe it or not. A jury will believe it."

"That's nice," Tragg said. "Now, while I may sound antagonistic and sarcastic at times, Perry, I try to be friendly, bearing in mind that we're on opposite sides of the fence. You didn't by any chance go to Paul Drake's office to get him to put out men looking for your client, Nancy Banks, did you?"

"I'm wondering where she is," Mason said.

"Quit wondering," Tragg told him. "She's boarding with us. She doubtless will be calling you on the telephone after she's been formally booked, but it won't do you any good to try to see her tonight. The offense for which she's arrested isn't bailable. For your information, she's being held on a charge of first-degree murder."

"I thought you'd turned her loose and told her not to leave town," Mason said. "What made you change your mind?"

"Rather a slick stunt you pulled," Tragg said, "sending

her out of the motel and following along behind to see if a police car might be following, but we were just a little ahead of you on that."

"What happened?" Mason asked.

"I'm afraid," Tragg said, "I'd be violating a professional confidence if I told you *exactly* what happened. Your client can tell you in the morning. All I'm telling you is where she is."

"You mean something else happened which caused you to charge her with murder?"

Tragg said, "Well, I don't ordinarily go around broadcasting information, Mason, but in this particular case *I* think you're sincere, even if the D.A.'s office doesn't. I don't think you had anything to do with it and perhaps you should start thinking about protecting yourself."

"Had to do with what?" Mason asked.

"The fact that while you were chaperoning your client and seeing there were no police cars following her, she turned off on the side road which went to the Osgood Trout Farm, stopped at the big litter can in front of the office and was busily engaged in pulling out dry ice containers when the police stepped up and asked her what she was doing."

"What did she say?" Mason asked.

Tragg said dryly, "She'd better tell you that herself. I've told you enough. The D.A.'s office is acting on the assumption that she went there at your suggestion to retrieve damaging evidence."

"And the police followed her there?" Mason asked.

"The police aren't quite that naïve," Tragg said. "When we found the dry ice container with part of a printed label still on it, we did a little research on the telephone, found out that these containers were printed for the Osgood Trout Farm. We had a radio car sent out to inspect the litter can. The officers found the discarded dry ice cartons all right, so I gave the men instructions to drive the police car off the road, conceal themselves in the brush and wait.

"That was why I took occasion to show you the fragment

of the dry ice receptacle, to question your client about it, and then tell you both you were free as air, just so your client didn't try to leave town.

"Of course the D.A.'s office is adopting the position that she told you where she had planted these receptacles, that you told her that was a dumb thing to do and to go and get them fast while you'd cover her rear to make certain that no police car was following."

"Well, thanks for the tip," Mason said.

"It's not a tip, it's a professional courtesy," Tragg said. "Thanks for phoning about Larsen Halstead. Keep him right there until my men show up. And for personal reasons I'm hoping, Perry, you weren't dumb enough to tell that girl to go get those containers. You should have more confidence in police efficiency than that."

"I *try* not to be naïve," Mason said.

"I'm satisfied you do," Tragg said, and hung up.

Within three minutes a uniformed police officer appeared at Drake's office. "Larsen Halstead?" he asked.

Halstead arose, nodded, said, "Here."

The police officer said, "You're to come with me."

"Very well, sir."

After Halstead left the office, Mason said, "I hope, Paul, you have that conversation recorded."

"Every word of it," Drake said. "Didn't you see me press the switch that turns on the tape recorder? What did Tragg say to you? You acted as though you'd had something of a jolt."

"I had something of a jolt," Mason said. "You can quit trying to find out anything about Nancy Banks. She's in jail charged with first-degree murder.

"I'm going home and try to get some sleep and you'd better do the same."

Chapter 11

A tearful Nancy Banks faced Perry Mason in the visitors' room at the county jail.

"I lied to you," she said. "I'm not worthy of your support. I know that you'll withdraw from my case and I can't help it. I don't blame you."

Mason said, "You're my client. I stick by my clients. You're also a damned fool. Now tell me what happened."

"I lied."

"I know you lied."

"I . . . I was trying to keep from being framed," she said, her lips quivering.

"Who was trying to frame you?"

"I don't know. All I know is that when I saw that dry ice packed around the body I knew what had happened. Someone had known about my theory of fooling the police on the time of death, and had framed me."

"When did you discover the dry ice?"

"A little while after I first discovered the body."

"And when was that?"

"Well, I went to the motel and I felt sure something was wrong. I'd left the door locked and I found the door unlocked. I had that uneasy feeling that someone was in there and I was frightened."

"I looked through the place and opened the bathroom door and . . . and then I saw it."

"All right. Then what did you do?"

"I went out to a telephone booth and called Mr. Drake's office again. After that I kept waiting there at the telephone booth until I got the message that you'd agreed to come."

"And then what?"

"Then I went back to the motel to wait for you. I sat outside in the car because I didn't want to go in and be alone with . . . with that thing."

"And then what?"

"Then I forced myself to go in and take a look and make sure he was dead. I began to have the most horrible feeling that perhaps he wasn't dead and I was sitting outside and letting him bleed to death or something."

"All right. You went inside. Then what?"

"I reached down to feel his pulse. My left hand encountered something cold as ice, and then I saw the dry ice, then I saw the Osgood Trout Farm on the label. That was when I got in a panic. I just went completely out of control. Why I did what I did I'll never know."

"Never mind that now," Mason said. "Just what did you do?"

"I picked up all the dry ice and ran out and put it in the automobile. I knew it was only about a five-minute ride to the trout farm and that there was a litter box outside of the trout farm. They use dry ice there at the trout farm and I felt certain if I put those boxes of dry ice in the litter box the dry ice would be evaporated before anyone had any occasion to see the packages, and that then it would naturally be assumed they had been packages that had been discarded by the trout farm."

"Go on," Mason said.

"I was just a nitwit. I forgot all about fingerprints. . . . Oh, Mr. Mason, if you'll just forgive me this time I swear— I promise I'll never, never deceive you again."

"Keep talking for a while," Mason said. "I have to know what happened."

"Well, when Lieutenant Tragg showed that there had been a piece torn from one ice container and you talked about my fingerprints I just went cold inside, something shriveled up inside of me. I remembered about the fingerprints for the first time. What you didn't know, but I did know, was that those Osgood Farm containers are printed with special advertising and I could see there was a little printing left on that piece of cardboard the officer was holding."

"He wanted you to see it," Mason said. "I told you it was a trap. He'd already staked officers out at the trout farm. You played right into his hands."

"I can see it all now. I was just dumb."

"Let's get back to what you did," Mason said. "You took the packages of dry ice, loaded them in your car, took them out and put them in the litter can."

"Yes."

"Just tossed them in on top?"

"No, I put my arm down and burrowed way down so they'd be down at the bottom where people wouldn't see them if they just happened to be looking. I didn't want a lot of partially empty packages to attract too much attention, and there were blood smears on two of the containers."

"Handling those containers," Mason said, "accounts for your hands being so cold when you came back to the motel."

"Yes. I tried to pass it off but . . . I hadn't realized just how cold my hands were."

"So then you remembered about the printed labels, the blood smears and possible fingerprints and decided that if the coast were clear and no police car was following you, you'd detour long enough to get those packages of dry ice."

"Yes."

"Then what were you going to do with them?"

"I was going to put them in a weighted sack and sink them in the deepest pool. I wanted to do something to remove my fingerprints. I felt the police would eventually find them all right and that was a risk I'd have to take. I didn't dare have them in my automobile and be stopped. So I just wanted to do something that would take my fingerprints off of those packages. I felt soaking them in that cold water would do the trick."

"You found all of the ten containers, and pulled them out?"

"Yes."

"All ten of them?"

"Yes."

"Including those with the blood smears?"

"Yes, all of them."

"Then what happened?"

"Then all of a sudden there was this dazzling light right in my eyes. A man had come up behind me. I hadn't heard him. The man in front of me put the flashlight right in my face and this man's voice said, 'We're officers, lady. Don't make a move.'"

"What did you do?"

"I screamed. I was so frightened, I—I've never felt like that before in my life. My soul just shriveled up inside of me. I just was crazy, I was so frightened."

"All right," Mason said, "you were caught red-handed. You had a feeling of guilt. You tried to justify yourself. Now, what did you say?"

"Mr. Mason, there wasn't anything I *could* say. I tried to think of something— I'd have given my right arm to have thought of a good lie, and I couldn't think of one to save my life. I was just trapped. I just stood there absolutely speechless."

"I know," Mason said, "but they didn't let you get away with that. They kept pressing you for an explanation. They asked you what you were doing there at that trash barrel. They told you to speak up. They told you that if you could make an explanation, they'd only be too glad to accept it; that they were just as anxious to have you cleared as you were to be cleared; that they knew from experience that many times a person did things which placed him in a guilty light, that a person quite frequently seemed to be guilty of something when, actually, there was a logical explanation for all of his actions."

"Mr. Mason!" she exclaimed. "Why, you know *exactly* what they said. How did you know?"

"It's a standard line of patter," Mason said. "What did you do? How did you respond? You must have tried to justify yourself."

"I just couldn't, Mr. Mason. There was nothing I could say. I just finally drew myself up and said that if they didn't have any more confidence in me than that, that any explanation I could make wouldn't do any good at all, and that they should see my lawyer."

"And they kept after you?"

"I'll say they kept after me. They interrogated me, they put me in an automobile, hustled me up to the jail, they had a matron come in, they questioned me in relays for hours, it seemed."

"What did you do?"

"I just sat tight. I had got to the point where I realized the more I said, the worse off I was going to be, so I decided to say nothing. I suppose that was the wrong thing to do."

"Under the circumstances, it was probably the best thing you could have done," Mason said, frowning thoughtfully as he contemplated the situation.

Abruptly, he said, "All right, now tell me why you bet on that horse in the first place. Where did the tip come from?"

"I didn't have any tip."

With an expression of annoyance, Mason got to his feet.

"All right, Nancy," he said, "I guess we had to come to a parting of the ways sometimes, but I've been lied to long enough. And may I say that, in my opinion, you're a very poor liar. I don't know whether it's because you haven't had enough practice, or whether it's because you have too poor an opinion of the intelligence of your audience. But you—"

"Mr. Mason, please, please," she said. "I'm telling you the truth. This is once I'm telling you absolutely the whole truth."

Mason said, "Don't be silly. You had some powerful,

compelling reason for betting on that horse. The horse was one that no one with inside information expected to win; otherwise, the odds wouldn't have been so great. When a young woman in your financial position goes out and puts five hundred dollars right on the nose of a long shot to win, she isn't just playing a hunch."

Mason started for the door.

"Wait, Mr. Mason. Wait. I'll tell you."

The lawyer paused, half turned.

"I didn't have any hunch, Mr. Mason. I didn't have any tip. I just . . . I just played him because . . . well, don't you see . . . he was the only horse I *could* have played."

"No, I don't see," Mason said.

"I hate to tell you this, Mr. Mason, because it reflects on someone else, but . . . well . . ."

"Go ahead," Mason said.

"It was Rod," she said.

"Rod?" Mason asked. "Your brother?"

"Yes. He . . . he had embezzled several thousand dollars and he couldn't make good, and someone had found out about the embezzlement."

"Who?" Mason asked.

"I think it was Mr. Halstead, the manager of the company. I don't know. I didn't find out who it was."

"How did you know your brother had embezzled money?"

"He told me over the telephone. He called me to say good-bye. He said that the next time I'd see him, he'd probably be in jail."

"And why did he call you to say good-bye? What did he want?"

"What makes you think he wanted anything?"

"I think he wanted something," Mason said. "What was it?"

"He wanted . . . money."

"How much?"

"Enough to cover his embezzlement."

"Did you give it to him?"

"No."

"Why?"

"I didn't have it to give."

"What did you do?"

"Mr. Mason, every cent I could raise was five hundred dollars. I had five hundred dollars put aside in a savings account. It had been four hundred and seventy-five and I had deposited twenty-five dollars out of my last paycheck, to make an even five hundred dollars. I swore that I wouldn't touch that, no matter what happened."

"What did you do?"

"I did the only thing I could do, Mr. Mason. There was only one way a girl in my position could make a large sum of money quick, and that was by taking the money to the track and putting it all on the nose of whatever horse seemed to have the biggest odds. That is, whatever horse would bring in enough odds in order to pay off."

"Why, you— Good heavens," Mason said. "You should have lost your— All right, go ahead. It sounds crazy, yet in one way, it's logical."

"Don't you see, Mr. Mason? It's absolutely logical. The five hundred dollars wouldn't have done me a bit of good. My brother needed the money. He needed a large sum of money, and he needed it right away. He needed it in the form of cash, and he needed it so that people wouldn't know he had received it. And . . . well, that's what I did. My brother told me he had been taking money out of the business from a secret cash drawer that he had found. I think he said a hidden cash drawer. I kept asking if he didn't mean petty cash, and he said no, it wasn't petty cash."

Mason's eyes narrowed thoughtfully. "I'm beginning to get a picture," he said. "Go ahead."

"Well, that's the story. That's all there was to it. I just

grabbed the cash and went down to the track and looked for a horse that had odds that would enable me to do some good if I won. I was perfectly miserable, Mr. Mason. To tell you the truth, I didn't dare hope that I stood even a slim chance of winning. But I knew the five hundred dollars would be no good to Rod, and I might just as well be broke as the way I was, as far as Rodney was concerned."

"That's a hell of a way to pick a horse," Mason said, "but, under the circumstances, it seems to have worked."

"It did work, Mr. Mason, and—"

"Now, wait a minute," Mason said. "Rodney bet fifty dollars on the same horse. How did that happen?"

"He used almost exactly the same form of reasoning I did," she said. "He had to have money and he had to have it fast, but he could only raise a limited amount. So he put fifty dollars on a long shot and fifty dollars on some hot tips he felt would win."

"Well, why didn't you make a fifty-dollar bet?" Mason asked.

"Because *I* needed enough to cover the shortage."

"How much was it?"

"Rodney told me it was about four thousand dollars."

"Then why not bet three hundred dollars on that horse and save two hundred for another long shot?"

"Because I know enough about racing to know that the odds that are posted are not determining, they're only an estimate of the odds, and the real odds are sometimes quite a bit different, particularly if a horse seems to have odds that are heavy enough so it attracts a lot of desperate people— that is, people who were in the same position I was in."

"And why didn't you cash in your tickets?" Mason asked.

She said, "I was at the racetrack. My brother didn't know it. He was there. I knew it. I saw him. And he had bet on the horse. I didn't know that until after the race, then I was so excited I was just trembling like a leaf. I started for the window where I would collect the hundred-dollar bets, and my brother was there, at the other window, and Mr. Fremont was there, also. They made a terrific scene. Mr. Fremont insisted that the money my brother had bet had been embezzled from him, and, therefore, he was entitled to all the winnings, and then it turned out he had a warrant for my brother's arrest and the officers were right there, and— Oh, it was terrible."

"Go on," Mason said.

"So I felt sure that they must have been watching that betting window and knew that I had put money on the horse, and—"

"Did Mr. Fremont know you personally?"

"Oh, yes. He knew me and didn't like me— That is, I mean, he . . . well, he liked me, but . . . I don't . . . didn't like him."

"Passes?" Mason asked.

"Passes and pawings," she said. "He started out with a sort of a paternal attitude. I was working for him, and he gave Rodney a job as a favor to me. For a while he'd be sort of pawing around and patting, and then he got to making deliberate passes."

"So you quit the job and stayed away from the office?"
"Yes."

"Your brother told you he'd embezzled money?"
"Yes."

"And he said how much?"

"Between thirty-five hundred and four thousand dollars."

"I understood the shortage was only a thousand or fifteen hundred dollars," Mason said.

She said, "At one time it was nearly five thousand. Then he made some winnings and reduced it greatly. But I knew how explosive the situation was. I wanted to have enough to get him in the clear on the embezzlement, then ease the financial pressure which had caused him to embezzle in the first place."

"And he couldn't pay off?"

"No, he was desperate. He was down to his last few hundred dollars, and— Well, I think he tried to embezzle more. I think he felt the same way that I did, that it was whole hog or nothing. And I think his idea was that he'd just as soon go up for embezzlement of five thousand dollars as for thirty-five hundred. But something had happened. I don't know what it was, but the cash wasn't available. Anyway, all he took was a hundred dollars when he went to the track. That was all the betting money he took."

Mason thought that over, suddenly said, "All right, Nancy, I'll tell you what to do. Just sit absolutely tight. Don't tell anybody anything. Don't give the police as much as the time of day. Now, they'll try to interrogate you. They'll sing you a very sweet story about how they think you're protecting someone else, and they want you to—"

"Oh, but they've done that already."

"And you didn't tell them anything about your brother?"

"I didn't tell them anything, period."

"Okay," Mason said. "Sit absolutely tight. Don't tell them anything except that I am representing you, that if they want any information they are to ask me, that I will release any statement that is to be made.

"Now there's one other thing I've got to warn you about, and that is the newspaper racket. Reporters and sob-sisters, specialty writers and all of that sort, will come asking you for an exclusive interview and telling you how much good it will do you and your case if you have a favorable newspaper background, and if you'll talk with them, they'll try to present you to the public in the most favorable light possible."

"And that will just be a lie?" she asked.

"Not necessarily," Mason said. "Some of those reporters are very square shooters. They don't try to take sides as far as the case is concerned, but they would try to give their readers a very sympathetic portrayal of you, of your life, of your character, of the dazed little girl who has never been in any trouble, who has always been a trusted secretary, who now finds herself sucked into a vortex of events over which she has no control and who is sitting in jail, awaiting trial on a charge of first-degree murder. And they'll describe you and your character, your reactions, and all you'll tell them about your love life and they'll pull a good sob-sister line that will tend to arouse public sympathy."

"But I'll have to talk first?"

"Usually. Sometimes they try to arouse sympathy just because it's good newspaper publicity. But usually you have to give them a story. And then they dress up the background."

"And I'm not to give them a story?"

"No matter what happens," Mason said, "you are to say absolutely nothing to anyone. Now, that is absolutely positive and absolutely final. Can you do that?"

"Yes."

"It's going to take nerves, guts and stubborn determination."

"I can keep quiet. I've put enough entries on the debit side of the ledger already. If you'll stay by me, Mr. Mason, I'll do what you tell me to."

"All right," Mason told her. "I've got work to do. One hell of a lot of work to do. You keep quiet—that's your share of the job at present."

The lawyer signaled to the matron that his visit was over, hurried down in the elevators to a phone booth and called Paul Drake.

When he had Drake on the line, Mason said, "This is Perry, Paul. Now, I've got a job for you."

"Shoot."

"It's against the law for anyone to take an inventory of the personal possessions of a dead man, or open safes or anything of that sort except in the presence of a representative of the State Inheritance Tax Appraiser's Office."

"So what?" Drake asked.

"So," Mason said, "the police will be going down to Fremont's office and taking an inventory of the cash in the safe and in a secret vault. They won't want to do it without notifying the State Inheritance Tax Appraiser, because they have a tip that there's a large sum of cash in that secret vault."

"Go on," Drake said.

"The State Inheritance Tax Appraiser will be asked to have a representative there. The police will be impatiently biting their fingernails until they get the red tape unwound."

"All right, how does that affect us?"

"It means," Mason said, "that I want to be present when that secret vault is opened."

"Not a chance," Drake said. "They wouldn't touch it with you there. The police would throw you out if you got within a block of the place. You're representing the defense and they don't intend to hand you all the evidence in advance and on a silver platter."

"They may not intend to," Mason said, "but they're going to. I happen to know that you've got some political pull with the State Inheritance Tax Appraiser. Ring up and say that you want me appointed as their representative, to be present at the time the place is opened and when they make an inventory."

"Why, Perry? They'll make an accurate inventory."

"I know they will," Mason said, "but I want to see what the place looks like. I want to get in there and I want to size up the whole situation before I get into court defending Nancy Banks on a charge of murder."

"It would put the Inheritance Tax Office in bad with the police if they did something like that," Drake said.

"Not necessarily," Mason said. "But give it a whirl, anyway."

"Well," Drake said dubiously, "I'll give it a whirl. I think I can put it across if I make it strong enough, if

. . . that is, if the law permits. And even if the law doesn't permit, I could give you some kind of a color of authority."

"That's all I need," Mason said, "a color of authority. I'm driving to the office. You get on the phone and try to have it fixed up by the time I get there."

Chapter 12

Mason fitted his key to the corridor door of his private office, clicked the lock back, opened the door and met Della Street's encouraging smile.

"How's everything coming?" she asked.

Mason shook his head. "I'm darned if I know, Della. When I'm with that girl, I believe her story. After I leave, I get to thinking she's the damnedest little liar I've ever met. Have we heard anything from Paul?"

"He wanted you to call as soon as you came in."

Mason nodded to her and she put through the call.

"He'll be down right away," she said. "What about the girl's story?"

"It's so wildly improbable," Mason said, "that it just doesn't make sense. I can just hear the district attorney's voice dripping sarcasm as he says, 'Now, Miss Banks, would you mind telling us that part once more, the part of your story where you were apprehended by the officers at the trash can, picking out the dry ice containers which you were afraid had your fingerprints on them. If you'll just clarify that phase of the case, I think I can conclude my cross-examination.'"

"That bad?" Della Street asked.

"Worse," Mason said.

Drake's code knock sounded on the door, and Della Street let him in.

Before the door had even been fully opened, Drake said, "I'm bringing bad news, Perry. I'm just tossing in my hat to see what happens."

"No dice with the Inheritance Tax Appraiser?"

"No dice. They couldn't do it, even if they wanted to, and they sure as hell don't want to—not with the district attorney's office in the picture."

Mason frowned and said, "They're going down there this morning to open up that secret receptacle where the cash is. They want to find out how much is there."

"What time will they go?"

"They've got to have a representative of the Inheritance Tax Appraiser there."

"I did that much," Drake said. "I got them to promise that they'd stall them off a little bit and give us a confidential ring to let us know just when the appraisal is going to take place. Of course, the police could just go down there at any time, looking for evidence instead of property."

"I know," Mason said, "but with a large sum of cash involved, the police are going to be just as cautious as the next person. The evidence will keep for a little while, and —What have you found out about Fremont, Paul?"

"Just the bare statistics. He was fifty-one years old, married, separated, no divorce, no children. He—"

"No divorce?" Mason interrupted.

"No divorce."

Mason snapped his fingers. "His widow," he said. "What do you have on her?"

"Inez Fremont," Drake said, reading from a notebook, "employed as cashier at the Grille & Cold Cafeteria, working at present from eight in the morning until four in the afternoon.

"She's ten or eleven years younger than he is. They were married three years ago. They separated a year ago. There's been no divorce."

Mason pushed back his chair. "Come on, Paul," he said, and then, after a moment, said to Della Street, "You'd better come along, too, Della. Bring a notebook, and, in taking down the things I say, be careful to note that I am *not* soliciting employment and that I tell her I *am* the attorney for the person who is charged with the death of her husband. Come on, let's go."

"Your car or mine?" Drake asked.

"Mine," Perry said. "I'll do the driving. You have the address of the cafeteria?"

"Right here," Drake said. "Do you want to phone first?"

Mason hesitated a moment, then said, "No, I think we'll try it cold turkey. She just might telephone the police that I was on my way down there, and the police would get ideas that I don't want them to have."

They hurried from the office down to Mason's car. The lawyer drove skillfully through traffic to the address Drake gave him. Their entrance to the cafeteria was during a slack period, as far as business was concerned. They approached the cashier's desk.

The blonde with steady, appraising gray eyes covered up the magazine she was reading as they approached the cashier's desk.

"May I be of assistance?" she asked.

"Are you Inez Fremont?" Mason asked.

There was a long moment of wooden-faced silence. Then she said, "Yes. What is it, please?"

"I'm Perry Mason," the lawyer said. "This is Della Street, my secretary, and I would like to introduce Paul Drake, a private detective.

"Now, I want to be absolutely fair and aboveboard, Mrs. Fremont. First, I think you should know that your husband is dead and—"

"I know all about that," she said. "The police have been here. They wanted to know if I had any information that would be of value."

"Did you?"

"No."

"You know about the circumstances of your husband's death?"

"Yes."

"This is a personal matter," Mason said. "But I understand that you were estranged?"

"Yes."

"Do you care to talk about it?"

"No."

Mason said, "Mrs. Fremont, I'm going to put my cards on the table. I am representing a young lady, Nancy Banks, who is at present accused of murdering your husband. I don't think she is guilty, but the circumstantial evidence is rather black against her. I am trying to get the facts. I don't want to do anything that would deceive you or to try to take advantage of you. But I would like to get some information from you, if you care to discuss it."

"If she killed him," Inez Fremont said shortly, "she deserves a medal."

"I don't think she killed him, Mrs. Fremont, but I must have all the information I can get in order to protect her interests and represent her."

"What do you want from me?"

"Mr. Fremont had been married before?"

"Not him."

"You had?"

"Yes."

"And that had broken up?"

"That's right."

Mason waited. She started to say something, then changed her mind, and after a few moments, the silence grew oppressive.

"There's nothing I can say that would help," Inez Fremont said at length.

"You have property rights," Mason said. "Have you consulted an attorney?"

"No property rights. I had to sign an agreement."

"What do you mean by saying you *had* to sign an agreement?"

"He forced me to."

"Could you perhaps tell me how?"

114

"Look, Mr. Mason," she said, "this whole thing is a pain in the neck to me. I want to forget it just as soon as I can."

"You were married three years ago?" Mason asked.

"Just about."

"And you were in love at that time?"

"Look, Mr. Mason, I'm forty years old and I look it. I've been knocked around in my life. I've reached a point where it's hard to get jobs. They want younger, more glamorous people. I'm an old workhorse. I want security. Every woman wants security. I thought I was getting it when I married this time, and I thought the man I was getting was in love with me."

"He wasn't?" Mason asked.

"Mr. Mason," she said, "it was a business marriage, as far as he was concerned."

Mason raised inquiring eyebrows.

Again there was a period of silence which was painfully prolonged. Then she said, "All right, there's no reason I can't tell you. He didn't care any more for me than that."

She held up her fingers and gave a derisive snap.

"Then why did he marry you?" Mason asked.

"He married me," she said, "because he was smart enough to know that in this state a wife can't testify against her husband. He married me because I had some information that would have sent him to prison. He married me because he was afraid he was going to get sent up for receiving stolen property, and by marrying me, he sealed my lips.

"I didn't know all that at the time. I found it out later."

"But you signed a property settlement agreement before you were married?" Mason asked.

"I signed a property settlement *after* the separation."

"Why?" Mason asked. "You certainly were entitled, under the circumstances, to—"

"It's a long story and a personal story," she said. "I was foolish. I didn't realize the type of man I was dealing with.

115

He was absolutely ruthless, unspeakably clever—clever isn't the word for it. Cunning is a better word.

"He keeps a detective agency working for him. It's an unscrupulous detective agency, but it's efficient. They kept on my trail from the minute I walked out of Fremont's house, only I didn't know it. They were clever enough so that I never suspected a thing. Fremont waited until he had some embarrassing things he could bring up, and then— well, he handled it in a very dramatic manner. . . . There's no need of going into all that, but, anyhow, I signed the property settlement."

Mason said, "Mrs. Fremont, I feel that I should tell you that right now you should get a lawyer. Don't put off for a minute. What time do you quit work?"

"Four o'clock this afternoon. I'm on from eight until four."

"Mrs. Fremont, *please* get yourself an attorney. Don't wait. Get on the telephone."

"What good could an attorney do?"

"An attorney might do a lot of good."

She shook her head. "An attorney would just cost me money."

Mason said, "Your husband is reported to have had a secret fund of cash. The police are going down there some time today to make an inventory of that money."

"It's his money. It wouldn't have anything to do with me."

"You can't tell what might turn up," Mason said. "I am not in a position to advise you, but, generally speaking, a contract which is entered into under duress, that is, where you are forced to sign a contract against your will or better judgment, can be declared invalid by the courts."

Her eyes showed a sudden sparkle of interest.

"How about you, Mr. Mason? I've heard about you. Would you look after my interests?"

"I would like to look after some of them," Mason said, after a moment's pause. "But I am representing Nancy

Banks on the murder charge. I couldn't have any interests that were in conflict with hers. If it should turn out, for instance, that you had murdered your husband, I would have to do everything I could to expose you, because I'm representing Nancy Banks and she is charged with murder."

Inez Fremont smiled a wan smile. "I *should* have killed him, but I didn't," she said.

Mason said, "I couldn't represent you, Mrs. Fremont, because in the first place, I have a primary loyalty to Nancy Banks. I want to keep myself free to do everything possible to help her and not have any other entangling alliances. I might want to adopt the position that you had murdered your husband."

"I only wish I had," she said. "He had it coming to him. I should have done it half a dozen times, but I didn't."

Mason said, "However, I do suggest that you get an attorney. I feel that it may be possible to uncover facts which will enable you to prove that that agreement which you executed was signed under duress. . . . Now, Mr. Drake here, as a detective, could attend the inventory-taking in your husband's office as your representative."

"Mr. Drake is in my employ as far as the murder is concerned and as far as getting facts about the murder is concerned, but there is no reason why he would be disqualified from getting facts in regard to material that was discovered in your husband's office, particularly anything that might show that the agreement you mentioned was entered into under duress."

"You think that agreement could be set aside?"

"I don't know," Mason said. "I'm not in a position to advise you. I simply suggest that you get a lawyer."

She turned to Paul Drake. "How much would it cost to have you present at the time they open my husband's office and inventory the contents and . . . well, keep your eyes open to see if you could find anything that would do like Mr. Mason says, in regard to that property settlement?"

Drake glanced at Mason, received an imperceptible nod.

"Not very much," Drake said. "It would cost you fifteen dollars."

She hesitated a moment, then opened her purse and handed the detective fifteen dollars.

"And you'll get an attorney?" Mason asked.

"I'll think it over," she said. "An attorney would want a retainer. Perhaps you don't realize just what fifteen dollars means to a working girl who is reaching an age where people look her over from head to foot when she makes an application for employment, and then start putting her off with excuses."

"All right," Drake said. "I'll try and be there and see what I can find out for you. If I can't do you any good, Mrs. Fremont, it won't cost you a penny."

"That's all right," she said. "I don't expect something for nothing. I've never had it yet, and I've been batting around for forty years."

Mason nodded to Della Street who hastily wrote out an authorization on a page of her notebook.

"Sign here," Drake said. "And I'll see what I can do."

Chapter 13

It was three o'clock in the afternoon when Drake returned to Mason's office with a report on the search of Fremont's office.

"What happened?" Mason asked.

"Well, it was the damnedest show you've ever seen."

"They had Halstead with them?"

"Sure."

"And he showed them the concealed vault?"

"That's right. There's a rug on the cement floor. The cement floor is divided into squares. You move the rug, and apparently there's nothing under it except the ordinary cement floor. But in the center square of the cement there's just a little, small square which fits in so tightly you can hardly see the mark where it joins. And where it joins is just the smallest place where you can insert a blade of a very thin screwdriver, if it has been ground down to almost razor thinness."

"Then what?" Mason asked.

"Then the square of cement comes up and discloses a ring, and you can take hold of that ring, and, by lifting, can pull the whole eighteen-inch square of cement right out, disclosing a metal box down underneath.

"Now, that cement union is so cunningly fitted that when the cement slab is put into place, it looks just exactly like the rest of the floor. The only thing that would have been a giveaway is this little square piece of cement on top. But the line of union there is just a hairline—and I mean a hairline. You have to look close to see it."

"But evidently Halstead had looked close."

"He'd looked close, probably because he was suspicious and was looking for something and knew what he was looking for."

"And Rodney Banks found it," Mason said.

"He probably found it, all right. But, remember, some of those people may have been surreptitiously watching Fremont.

"That office is the darnedest place I've ever seen. It has bars on the windows, and the door has a great big, heavy iron bolt, in addition to a lock. The walls are thick and it wouldn't surprise me at all if the windows had bulletproof glass."

"All that can keep," Mason said. "How much was in the secret place of concealment?"

Drake said, "Now there's the thing that is going to knock you for a loop, Perry. There wasn't a damned cent."

"What!"

"Nothing. It had been cleaned out, slick as a whistle."

"How come?" Mason asked.

"That's anybody's guess. But I can tell you something. The police weren't surprised."

"The hell they weren't.

"No, sir. Tragg took it right in his stride. He'd either been in there before and had made an investigation and found nothing was there, or else they're working on some theory of the case indicating that the money had already been taken out by somebody.

"The man who was surprised was Larsen E. Halstead. He took one look, then dropped down on his hands and knees and looked as though he couldn't believe his eyes, and then started to feel around with the tips of his fingers, but Tragg stopped him. He wanted to dust the interior of the steel container that was just under the slab of cement and which evidently had held the money, for fingerprints."

"How deep?" Mason asked.

"Probably about eighteen inches," Drake said. "I didn't

measure it. It may have been fifteen, it may have been twenty. But I'd say somewhere around eighteen inches."

"And the cement cover is eighteen inches square?"

"Yes. The cement floor has been scored into square lines so that the floor consists of lines eighteen inches square, and this looked exactly like any of the other places, except that it was a removable slab."

"And Tragg wasn't surprised?"

"Never turned a hair, Perry. He looked down at the empty receptacle, and I caught that sort of a foxy smile that sometimes twists the corners of his mouth. But Halstead said, 'What in the world,' and went down to his knees as though someone had clubbed him. Then he started reaching for the inside of the receptacle and Tragg grabbed his arm and said, 'No fingerprints, please.' "

"What did Halstead say?"

"Halstead looked up at him and said, 'It doesn't make any difference. My prints are there already. I had looked at the money and counted it. I knew it was there.' "

"And Tragg said?" Mason asked.

"Tragg just smiled that foxy smile and said, 'Well, Mr. Halstead, we won't leave any *more* of your fingerprints here and we'll try not to smudge or obliterate the prints anyone else may have left here.' "

"Then what?"

"They made an inventory of the office and the stuff in it, just sort of a general running inventory, and locked the place up again. But they took Halstead with them. They want to get some more information out of him on some phase of the case that I couldn't figure out."

"Did they make any trouble about you being there?" Mason asked.

"They all but bodily threw me out. Then I showed them the written authorization from Mrs. Fremont, told them I was representing the widow, and one of the cops accused me of sharp practice. I told him nothing of the sort, there was no reason I couldn't do investigative work for you and, at the same time, represent other clients. And then Tragg called them all to one side, they had a brief conference, and after that, Tragg came over and said that he appreciated my position, that he knew I was a square shooter and an ethical investigator and that they were not going to make any objection to my presence.

"Then Tragg went on to say that they hoped I would point out to Mrs. Fremont that they had extended every courtesy to her representative, that they were just as anxious as she was to get things cleaned up, and that any person representing her would be extended every possible courtesy by the police."

"Well, I'll be darned," Mason said. "There's something back of all this that we don't know. The police have other information we don't have."

"Is that surprising?" Drake asked.

"Not in this case," Mason said.

"Well," Drake told him, "that's the way it stands to date. Do you know anything more at your end?"

"They're having a hearing before the grand jury," Mason said. "They're going to indict Nancy Banks for first-degree murder and move the case right on to trial. A preliminary hearing might slow things down a bit—or so they think. They want to have a grand jury indictment, and then try to get an immediate trial."

"And you, of course, will try for delay?" Drake asked.

Mason said, "I'm going to look the evidence over pretty carefully. I'll get a transcript of the witnesses who testify before the grand jury, and I just may fool them, Paul."

"How?"

"Ever see a tug-of-war?" Mason asked. "Where the other side suddenly gives a lot of slack, and then, when their opponents have fallen all over themselves, reels in the line as easily as though there weren't any opposition? Well, I intend to give Hamilton Burger, our beloved district attorney, a lot of slack."

"How much slack?" Drake asked.

"All he needs to have is enough rope to hang himself," Mason said.

"That can be dangerous," Drake warned. "Hamilton Burger is a tough, resourceful fighter. If he doesn't have the facts to back him up, he can't win cases. But if he has the facts, he can fight his weight in wildcats and come out on top."

"I know," Mason said thoughtfully. "But I'm toying with an idea."

Chapter 14

Judge Navarro Miles regarded Hamilton Burger, the district attorney, thoughtfully. "The peremptory is with the defendant."

Mason arose. "If the Court please, we do not desire to exercise any peremptory challenge at this time. The jury is entirely satisfactory to the defense."

"Very well. The jury will be sworn," Judge Miles said.

The jurors rose collectively, held up their right hands and were sworn to well and truly try the case and the issues between the State of California, on the one hand, and Nancy Banks, on the other.

Judge Miles looked at Hamilton Burger thoughtfully. "Do I understand that the district attorney intends to appear personally in this case?"

"Yes, Your Honor. I will be assisted by my trial deputy, Robert Calvert Norris, who is here in court with me. But, for the most part, I intend to handle the case myself."

Judge Miles's expression revealed his curiosity.

"As a matter of fact," Hamilton Burger went on, "for reasons which will appear as the case develops, this is going to be a very important case and a unique case and one in which it will be necessary for the duly elected district attorney of this county to take a personal part. There are legal issues involved which will probably establish a precedent in this county.

"Now, if the court please, my associate, Mr. Norris, will make an opening statement to the jury."

"Very well, proceed," Judge Miles said.

Norris, a tall, slender individual with long, wavy auburn hair, large, blue eyes and a carefully dignified manner, strode forward to stand before the jury.

"If the Court please, and you, ladies and gentlemen of the jury," he said, "this is going to be a very short opening statement. I am going to outline only the facts that the prosecution expects to prove and our theory of the case."

He paused, squared his shoulders, looked solemnly and impressively at the jurors, and then went on.

"We expect to show that the defendant's brother, Rodney, was employed by the decedent, Marvin Fremont, and had embezzled a considerable sum of money from his employer. Most of this money had been bet on race horses.

"Fremont discovered the embezzlement and followed Rodney Banks to the track, where he found he had made a bet on a certain horse named Dough Boy, a long shot, that came in a winner.

"When Banks endeavored to collect his bet, Marvin Fremont insisted that the bet had been made, not with Rodney Banks's money but with Fremont's money, and, therefore, Fremont was entitled to the money.

"Banks was arrested for embezzlement.

"That, ladies and gentlemen of the jury, set the stage for murder.

"We are not going to try to tell you that Marvin Fremont, the dead man, was an angel. He wasn't. In fact, the evidence will show very much to the contrary.

"Fremont engaged in illicit transactions. For that purpose, he had a large sum of money which he kept concealed in his office.

"Rodney Banks, the brother of the defendant, had discovered that place of concealment. When Banks realized that his embezzlement had been detected, he played his trump card, feeling that he might as well be hanged for a sheep as a goat, as the saying goes. He was released on bail, promptly went to the office, cleaned out every bit of money there was in the secret cash and intended to use that as a bargaining weapon.

125

"Knowing that Fremont couldn't disclose the amount of his hidden cash without accounting for the reason it was there, knowing that Fremont would be inclined to bargain if the embezzling employee was in a bargaining position, Rodney Banks calmly took *all* of the money.

"That caused Marvin Fremont to look up the defendant, where she was registered at the Foley Motel, which was near a place known as the Osgood Trout Farm.

"This trout farm consisted of a privately operated series of pools stocked with trout and connected by a stream. Fishermen were given the opportunity to fish in the pool and stream and were charged for each trout that they caught.

"This trout farm was known to Lorraine Lawton, a friend of the defendant's who worked there, and to the defendant who sometimes helped out at the pool by donning an eye-catching bathing suit.

"In order to let sportsmen take their trout home without spoiling, the pool had a stock of dry ice.

"The defendant had keys to all of these facilities.

"The defendant went to the Foley Motel. She intended to meet her brother there. Fremont was having her shadowed. He knew where she was.

"We now come to a chapter in the case which we would like to avoid, if possible, but in all frankness, ladies and gentlemen of the jury, we cannot avoid it.

"Not only did Rodney Banks bet with embezzled money, but he gave some of this embezzled money to his sister, with instructions to bet on the horse, Dough Boy. The sister made five one-hundred-dollar bets on this horse. But when she saw her brother arrested when he tried to cash in his tickets, she left the track in a panic, went to the office of Perry Mason and gave him the tickets to cash in the next day.

"Mr. Mason did cash in those tickets and took them to the defendant at the motel, despite having been put on notice that the tickets had been purchased with embezzled money.

"Marvin Fremont came to the motel. He was probably

abusive. The post-mortem shows that he had been drinking heavily. The defendant shot him there. The body was in the shower bath.

"We now come to an interesting phase of the case, where the defendant, trying to conceal the crime and knowing that the police fix the time of death by taking the body temperature, decided to alter the time element so that it would appear the murder had been committed at a much earlier hour.

"The defendant went to the Osgood Trout Farm nearby, secured a large quantity of dry ice and literally packed the body of the decedent in dry ice. Then she waited for the body temperature to be lowered by this means, and when she felt it had been effective, telephoned her attorney, Perry Mason, asking him to come to the motel.

"When she was assured Perry Mason was on the way, and knowing that the containers of dry ice had had an opportunity to do their work, she picked up these containers, took them back to a trash barrel at the Osgood Trout Farm and deposited them there.

"The evidence will also show you, ladies and gentlemen of the jury, that, alarmed when the dry ice trick had been discovered, she returned to the trash barrel for a purpose which the evidence will disclose and which led to the discovery of one of the most important pieces of circumstantial evidence in the case.

"On the strength of this evidence, ladies and gentlemen of the jury, the prosecution will ask for a verdict of first-degree murder. Murder with premeditation aforethought. Murder with malice. Murder with deliberation. Murder for greed and to conceal a crime.

"At the conclusion of this evidence, I think you will agree the prosecution has established its case beyond all reasonable doubt.

"I thank you."

Robert Norris turned and walked back to the prosecution's table.

Hamilton Burger, the district attorney, made no secret of his feeling that the opening argument had been well done. He shook hands with his trial deputy and smiled beamingly at him.

Judge Miles said to Perry Mason, "Does the defense wish to make an opening statement at this time?"

"The defense will reserve its opening statement," Mason said.

"Very well. Call your first witness," Judge Miles said.

Robert Norris, taking charge of the preliminary details, called a surveyor and introduced a map of the premises, showing the distance by highway from Osgood Trout Farm to the Foley Motel, a distance of not over a mile and a half. The map was introduced as the prosecution's exhibit M1.

He called the autopsy surgeon, who testified that death had been virtually instantaneous and had been caused by a bullet from a .38-caliber revolver which penetrated the heart.

While this witness was being interrogated as to the anatomical details, Mason turned to Nancy Banks and whispered, "Nancy, you must tell me the truth. Did you participate, with your brother, in an embezzlement?"

"No."

"What bit of evidence did they recover from the trash barrel at the Osgood Trout Farm which is intended to surprise us?"

"The dry ice containers," she whispered.

Mason shook his head. "They know all about those and know that we know all about them. This is something they know about which we *don't* know about."

"I don't know," she said. "There couldn't have been anything."

"No further questions," Robert Norris announced dramatically. "You may cross-examine."

Mason patted Nancy Banks reassuringly on the shoulder, rose and regarded the witness.

"Doctor, you have testified that you recovered the fatal bullet?"

"Yes, sir."

"And turned it over to the police?"

"Yes, sir."

"Where did you recover it?"

"From a corner of the shower bath, where the body was slumped and where it had fallen after being shot."

"You turned this bullet over to the Police Ballistics Department?"

"Yes, sir. I turned it over to Lieutenant Tragg of Homicide, and I believe he turned it over to Ballistics."

"Now then," Mason said, "how did you know it was the fatal bullet?"

The doctor smiled. "It was the only bullet in the shower, and the bullet had gone clean through the body."

"How do you know the man was killed in the shower bath?" Mason asked.

"Because death was instantaneous, and that was where he fell."

"How do you know he fell there?"

"The body was recovered there."

"The bullet had gone entirely through the body?"

"Yes."

"And was found in the shower bath as a spent bullet?"

"Yes, sir."

"So," Mason said, "you, being called to examine the body, deduced that the man must have been shot at the place where he was found and deduced that the bullet, which was found in the shower bath, must have been the fatal bullet?"

"Well, those were natural assumptions."

"In other words," Mason said, "you're testifying to assumptions and not to facts."

"Well, I think they're logical assumptions."

"Your thoughts in the matter are not binding upon the defendant. The defendant is bound only by facts. Now, then, you don't know that the man whose body you found in the shower bath was killed there, do you?"

"Well, I certainly—No, I don't *know* it. I wasn't there at the time of the shooting."

"Exactly. For all you know, the body may have been shot outside of the motel, taken into the shower and placed there."

"That would hardly be a logical assumption."

"But it's a possible assumption. Answer the question yes or no. It's a possibility?"

"Yes, it's a possibility."

The witness hesitated a moment and said, "But it isn't a logical possibility."

"Why not?"

"There was no blood on the floor. The only blood was in the shower bath. Powder burns show the shot was fired within about three inches of the body. It would have been difficult for anyone to have transported the corpse, and it would have been impossible for a young woman, such as the defendant, to have carried the corpse across the motel to the shower bath."

"Therefore, assuming that the defendant was the one who committed the crime, you assume that the body couldn't have been carried across the room?" Mason asked.

"That's what I just said."

"You're relying on a lot of surmises and testifying, not as to facts, Doctor, but as to conclusions. Your premise is that the defendant fired the fatal shot. Assuming that, you reach conclusions as to the evidence."

"Well, they're logical conclusions. You can't explain the facts by any other logical means."

"And why would the decedent have walked into the motel room, stalked past the defendant and gone directly into the shower?"

"That I can't tell you."

"Can you suggest any logical reason?"

"I don't have to. I'm here to testify as to facts, not to surmises as to what may have happened."

"Yet your entire testimony is a mass of surmises as to what has happened," Mason said. "I move to strike the testimony of this witness from the record, if the Court please."

Judge Miles said, "The motion is denied, but the jury is instructed to pay no attention to the conclusions of the witness as to what must have happened. The jury will take only the testimony of this witness in regard to basic facts and technical conclusions as to medical facts which are within the province of expert testimony. The Court will strike out all of the other testimony and instruct the jury to disregard it."

"Including the testimony about the fatal bullet?" Mason asked.

"Certainly," Judge Miles said. "This witness doesn't know it was the fatal bullet. The prosecution is entitled to show the presence of the body in the shower. It is entitled to show the cause of death. It is entitled to show the presence of *a* bullet in the shower. It is entitled to show that that was the *only* bullet in the shower. As far as the rest is concerned, those are conclusions for the jury to draw, not the witness."

"Oh, if the Court please," Hamilton Burger said, "I feel that my learned friend here has carried technicalities too far."

"Well, the Court feels that the witnesses should testify to facts, not to conclusions," Judge Miles snapped. "The ruling stands."

"I don't think, if the Court please, that the Court is entitled to sift the testimony of a witness in this way and tell the jurors what parts it can regard and what parts it cannot regard."

"The ruling goes further than that," Judge Miles said. "I have striken the balance of the evidence.

"Now, Mr. Prosecutor, I am trying to save time. If you

want to be technical about the power of the Court, I will grant the defense motion and strike out all of the testimony on the ground that it is based on conclusions, then you can re-question the witness as to the matters on which he can properly testify, the finding of the body, the cause of death, the powder burns, the presence of a bullet—not in the body but in the shower."

"Very well," Hamilton Burger said, with poor grace. "I find myself in a position where I must, of course, accept the Court's ruling and respect it. But may I respectfully point out that Mr. Mason had his opportunity to object to the questions as I asked them.

"In other words, I asked the doctor if he had found the fatal bullet and he said he had. At that time, if the Court please, Mason had every opportunity to object that the bullet was not the fatal bullet; or, rather, that the witness had no means of knowing that it was the fatal bullet."

"You chose to put on your case by asking questions which called for conclusions of the witness," Judge Miles said. "I would be inclined to go along with your comments in regard to the tactics of defense counsel, were it not for the fact that the Court felt you noticed a whispered conference from time to time between counsel and the defendant, and tried to take advantage of preoccupation on the part of the defense counsel by asking questions which were so planned as to call for a conclusion of the witness."

"I didn't ask those questions," Hamilton Burger said.

"Your office did. You're responsible. Now, proceed with the case."

Burger, his color indicating his indignation, slowly sat down.

"Call Lieutenant Tragg to the stand," Robert Norris said.

Tragg came forward with urbane geniality, his manner that of a man who is employed by the taxpayers and is doing the duty which the taxpayers hired him to perform.

Lt. Tragg testified to receiving a telephone call from Perry Mason indicating that a body had been discovered in the shower bath in the motel room of his client, the defendant in this action; that Tragg had proceeded at once to the premises, and there found the body; that, in company with the doctor who had just testified, he had examined the body; that, in the shower bath, they had found one bullet and only one bullet; that he had that bullet with him. He produced the bullet, which was introduced in evidence.

The Lieutenant stated that he had turned that bullet over to the Ballistics Department, that he had been with the Ballistics Department when tests were made to determine whether that bullet had been fired from one certain .38-caliber revolver, that the tests had proven the bullet had been fired from that revolver, that he had that revolver with him and would produce it, to be received in evidence.

Mason turned to Nancy. "Where did they get that gun?" he asked.

"I don't know," she whispered. "*I* never saw it."

"We ask that this gun be introduced in evidence," Norris said.

"Just a minute," Mason announced, getting to his feet. "I have some questions on the *voir dire*."

"Very well," Judge Miles ruled. "You may interrogate the witness on the *voir dire* in regard to this weapon, Mr. Mason."

"Where did you get this weapon?" Mason asked.

Lt. Tragg's face was positively cherubic. "It was handed me by a police officer."

"Do you know where the police officer got it?"

"Only by hearsay," Tragg said. "And, of course, I couldn't testify as to hearsay evidence."

"You personally participated with the ballistics expert in testing this gun and this bullet which was recovered from the shower bath?"

"I did, yes, sir."

"And you are, I believe, an expert in regard to firearms identification?"

"I consider myself as such, although I am not the official

police expert. However, I was present when the tests were made by a comparison microscope testing the bullet, which I will refer to as the shower bullet, rather than the fatal bullet, with a test bullet fired from this weapon which I am holding in my hands. I checked the comparison microscope and have no hesitancy in stating that, in my opinion, this shower bullet was fired from this weapon I am holding in my hand and from no other weapon."

"You traced the registration of this weapon from its numbers?" Mason asked.

"I did, yes, sir."

"And who purchased that weapon? To whom was it registered?"

"The weapon," Tragg said, smiling affably, "was purchased by Marvin Fremont. It was a weapon described in a permit which we found on Mr. Fremont's person at the time of his death."

"In other words, Fremont had purchased this gun, made an application for a permit to carry it on the grounds that he had to carry large sums of cash at times and wanted personal protection?"

"Exactly."

"And received a permit on that basis?"

"That's right."

"And you don't know where this weapon was found?" Mason asked.

"Only by hearsay," Tragg said, beaming.

Mason turned to the Court. "That's the conclusion of my questioning on *voir dire*, if the Court please. I have no objection to receiving the weapon in evidence."

Mason sat down, turned to Nancy Banks, whispered, "Nancy, that was what they found in the trash container out at the Osgood Trout Farm."

"No, no," she whispered back, her eyes wide with alarm. "It couldn't have been . . . it—"

"Just what do you think you can accomplish by lying to me all the time and putting me in a situation where I am fighting blind?" Mason asked irritably. "Now, I'm going to do the best I can to help you, but I'm tired of your lies."

"Now, what else did you find, Lieutenant?" Norris asked after the formalities of putting a tag on the gun and introducing it as People's Exhibit "B" were concluded.

"In putting my hands under the body," Lt. Tragg said, "I noticed that the tile floor of the shower was cold, very, very cold."

"You expected to find the floor of the shower cool because of evaporation of moisture and because of the tile?"

"I did."

"And this was cooler than you had anticipated?"

"Much cooler. Moreover, the garments of the decedent were quite cold to the touch."

"Cool?"

"I said cold."

"And what did you do, with reference to investigating this matter of temperature?"

"The doctor had his clinical thermometer with him, for the purpose of testing body temperatures, and there was a thermometer in the motel. I used the thermometer in the motel. By putting it on the tile floor, I got a reading of forty degrees Fahrenheit. By putting it in the clothes of the decedent, I got a reading of forty-three degrees Fahrenheit. The temperature in the room itself was seventy-three degrees Fahrenheit."

"According to that same thermometer?"

"Yes, sir."

"Did you subsequently test that thermometer to determine its accuracy?"

"I tested the thermometer within an hour, after returning to Police Headquarters."

"And what did you find?"

"I found the thermometer was reasonably accurate, within a small but completely permissible variation."

"Did you find anything else?"

"Yes, I did. After my attention was attracted by the very

unusual clothing temperature and the temperature of the shower, I explored further and found a piece of pasteboard torn from a container."

"Do you have that pasteboard here?"

"I do."

Tragg produced the torn piece of pasteboard, introduced it in evidence.

"Then what did you do?"

"Then," Tragg said, "I went outside the motel, to the place where Perry Mason and his client, the defendant in this case, were waiting, and I told both of them that this piece of paper was, in my opinion—"

"Now, just a moment," Norris interrupted. "I don't want your opinion at this time. I only want to know what you *told* the defendant and her attorney, Perry Mason. I want to know just what you *said* in their presence."

"Yes, sir, I understand. I stated to them, and both of them, that in my opinion this piece of pasteboard was a fragment torn from a carton of dry ice, and I asked both of them if they knew anything about it."

"And what was said?"

"The defendant shook her head in the negative and then her attorney cautioned her to say nothing, not even to move her head."

"I think, if the Court please," Norris said, "that this concludes my direct examination of this witness at this time. I will probably want to recall him later, in connection with another phase of the case, but, at the moment, this is as far as I care to go. I turn the witness over to the defense for cross-examination."

Lt. Tragg, a dangerous antagonist, turned to face Perry Mason, his eyes wary but his smile friendly, his manner outwardly courteous.

Mason, realizing the trap which had been baited for him, was equally suave. "If the Court please, in view of the fact that the prosecution apparently intends to recall this witness at a later date to testify to further matters, I feel that it would be better for me to withhold my cross-examination and make it all at one time. If, of course, the prosecution does not recall him, as it has promised to do, I then reserve the right to recall the witness myself for cross-examination."

"Very well," Judge Miles said. "That seems fair. Call your next witness, Mr. Prosecutor."

Norris was unable to conceal his disappointment. He frowned angrily, turned in his chair to have a whispered conversation with Hamilton Burger.

Burger, however, courtroom veteran that he was, realizing the manner in which Norris was damaging his case by showing that Mason's tactics had him bothered, pushed Norris gently away and said, "The next witness for the prosecution will be Stanley Moulton."

The word was relayed to the corridor. "Stanley Moulton," a voice outside the door called.

A moment later, Moulton, who had been waiting in the witness room, stepped through the folding doors into the courtroom and walked to the witness stand.

Moulton, the preliminary questioning developed, was a police officer who had, on the evening of the third, the date of the murder, been assigned to duty in a radio patrol car.

Asked if he had received certain instructions, without specifying what those instructions were, he stated that he *had* received specific instructions. Asked what he did next, he stated he had gone at high speed to the vicinity of the Osgood Trout Farm, parked his car down a side street, walked back to take up a location in the brush, within some thirty feet of a trash barrel which was located there.

"Now then," Norris asked, "did you see the defendant on that night?"

"I did."

"Where?"

"At the trash barrel."

"Were you alone at the time?"

"No, sir. Another officer was with me."

"Now, what time did you see the defendant?"

"We first saw her at ten-sixteen. We took her into custody at ten-twenty-one."

"What did the defendant do at that time and place?"

"She drove up in an automobile, parked her car so that the headlights were shining on the trash barrel, left the motor running, got out of the car, looked around, stood, apparently in an attitude of listening, and went directly to the trash barrel."

"What did she do there?"

"She took out several articles from the trash barrel, then started pulling out pasteboard cartons. These cartons were, as it turned out, partially filled with dry ice."

"You didn't know that at the time?"

"Not at that *exact* moment, no. We found it out within a matter of minutes, however."

"Now, you say she pulled out these cartons?"

"Yes."

"Was there any carton that had a particular tear in it?"

"There was."

"That was one of the cartons taken by the defendant?"

"It was."

"And did you take that carton into your possession?"

"I did."

"Now, what did you do with that carton, with reference to it, and with reference to the torn piece of pasteboard, which has previously been introduced in evidence by Lieutenant Tragg as having been found under the body of the decedent, and which piece of pasteboard was introduced in evidence as People's Exhibit 'C'."

"You mean at a later date?"

"Yes, subsequent to the arrest, Mr. Moulton. In other words, I am simply trying to lay a foundation here."

"I see. I tested the two, to see if they matched."

"Now, you have the pasteboard carton, that is, the torn carton, which you recovered from the defendant there on the evening of the third?"

"Yes, sir."

"Will you produce it, please."

The witness opened a briefcase and took out a torn oblong carton.

"Now then, Mr. Moulton," Norris said, "I hand you the torn piece of pasteboard, which has been received in evidence as People's Exhibit 'C.' I am going to ask you to show to the Court Exhibit 'C' and this carton which you recovered, and show whether the torn piece, which has been received as Exhibit 'C,' matches the tear in the carton."

"Yes," the witness said, and matched the two pieces of pasteboard, taking care to handle the carton in such a way that the jurors could see that the torn fragment of pasteboard fitted perfectly into the torn carton.

"Now then, if the Court please," Norris said, "I ask that this carton be introduced in evidence as People's Exhibit 'D'."

Judge Milcs looked at Mason inquiringly.

Mason, knowing that the eyes of the jurors were on him, that this damning piece of evidence linked the defendant to the murder as no other bit of circumstantial evidence could have done, tried to make his voice sound indifferent, almost bored.

"Why, certainly, Your Honor. The defense has no objections. We will stipulate it may be received in evidence."

"So ordered," Judge Miles said. "It will be received in evidence as People's Exhibit 'D.'"

"Now then," Norris said, "if the Court please, I ask that the jurors be permitted to take Exhibit 'D' and Exhibit 'C' in their own hands at this time and see how the two pieces match."

"No objection whatever," Mason said, before Judge Miles could rule. "We're quite willing to have the jurors see the two pieces of evidence at this time."

Mason's voice and manner indicated that this came as no surprise to him, that he had anticipated it all along, that it was, after all, a matter of no moment.

The jurors, however, taking the two pieces of paper,

seeing how the torn pasteboard of Exhibit "C" fitted absolutely into the piece torn from the carton, Exhibit "D," looked significantly at each other, and one or two of them nodded thoughtfully, indicating that the evidence had made a deep and lasting impression.

When the jurors had returned the exhibits, Robert Norris, realizing, as did everyone in the courtroom, what he had accomplished with this dramatic presentation of the physical evidence, said, "Now, Mr. Moulton, I want to ask you what you did after you took the defendant into custody—immediately after you took her into custody."

"Well, we advised her that we were going to have to take her to Headquarters on suspicion of first-degree murder."

"What did she say, if anything?"

"She said that she had no comment to make, that Perry Mason was her lawyer, that she would say absolutely nothing, that if we wanted to know anything about the case, we would have to call on Perry Mason."

"So then what did you do?"

"We put her in the police car with my associate, and I returned to the trash barrel to look further."

"And you did look further?"

"I did."

"Did you find anything?"

"I did."

"Where?"

"At the very bottom of the trash barrel."

"What was it?"

"A .38-caliber revolver."

"I ask you if you took the number of that revolver."

"I did."

"And I ask you to examine the gun which has been introduced as People's Exhibit 'B' and compare the number of that gun with the number of the gun which you discovered."

The witness took a notebook from his pocket, accepted

the gun, made quite a show of studying each digit of the numbers carefully, then looked up and nodded.

"What is your finding?" Norris asked.

"The numbers match. That is the gun I recovered from the trash barrel."

"In other words, the gun which you found at the bottom of the trash barrel is the same gun which has been introduced in evidence as People's Exhibit 'B'?"

"It is."

Norris smiled triumphantly.

"What was the condition of the gun when you found it, Mr. Moulton?"

"The gun had one empty cartridge underneath the hammer. The other spaces in the cylinder were occupied by loaded cartridges."

"Well, Mr. Moulton, you are familiar with firearms. It is part of your police training to take a course in the handling of firearms, is it not?"

"Yes."

"And you are familiar with this particular make of weapon, a Smith & Wesson .38-caliber revolver?"

"I am, yes, sir."

"And this empty cartridge which you mentioned finding, you say was under the firing pin?"

"That is right. The revolver was a double-action, self-cocking revolver. The empty cartridge was in the firing position. In other words, the gun had been, at one time, fully loaded with six shells. One of them had been discharged, and that one shell was in the same position in which it had been when it was fired. In other words, it was directly aligned with the barrel of the gun."

"Cross-examine," Norris said triumphantly.

"Why," Mason said, as though surprised at the very suggestion there should be a cross-examination, "we have no questions of this witness."

"No cross-examination?" Norris asked incredulously.

"Certainly not," Mason snapped.

"Call your next witness," Judge Miles said.

Hamilton Burger looked significantly at the clock.

"Well," Judge Miles amended, "it is approaching the hour of the afternoon adjournment. I believe Court will take its evening recess at this time.

"Ladies and gentlemen of the jury, the Court is not ordering you kept in custody but is releasing you to go to your homes—in this state, the Court having that option.

"However, the Court cautions you that you are not to discuss this case with anyone, or among yourselves. You are not to permit it to be discussed in your presence, you are not to read newspapers, you are not to listen to any radio or television account of the trial, you are not to form or express any opinion until the case is finally submitted to you for consideration.

"Court is adjourned until nine-thirty tomorrow morning."

Mason surreptitiously heaved a deep sigh and relaxed his hands, which had been tightly clenched with nervous tension.

Chapter 15

Perry Mason, Della Street and Paul Drake sat in the lawyer's office.

The atmosphere was thick with gloom.

Drake said, "I'm sorry Perry, but I can't uncover a darned thing that's going to help. As a matter of fact nothing is going to help. This is the sort of case that district attorneys dream about. Here Burger has pieces of circumstantial evidence that can't be questioned—the bullet out of the gun, the torn piece out of the dry ice container, the linking of them to the defendant by having her get caught red-handed planting the gun in the trash barrel."

Mason tilted back in his chair, his chin sunk on his chest, and kept his eyes fixed thoughtfully on the desk blotter.

Della Street, looking from Mason to Drake, then back to Mason, had eyes that were warm with sympathy for her employer's predicament.

"It isn't all a bed of roses for Hamilton Burger," Mason said. "There are some things that just don't make sense in connection with his theory."

"Don't worry about his *theory*," Drake said. "He's given you only the first barrel today. Tomorrow he's going to give you the second barrel. And there's gossip around the courthouse that the second barrel is really a humdinger. He's got you dead to rights. That's why he's sitting in on the case personally. He's going to enjoy his triumph to the limit."

Mason said, "Why would Fremont have gone into the girl's shower?"

"Beause she trapped him in there," Drake said.

"How would he have surrendered possession of the gun? It was a gun that he customarily carried."

"Carried where?" Drake asked.

"Probably in his hip pocket," Mason said. "Or, rather, he probably had a specially designed pocket tailored in his waistband, since it was a gun he carried all the time."

Drake said, "She could have pulled the old feminine sob-sister stuff on him, praying for mercy, throwing her arms around him, perhaps getting down on her knees and getting her hand under his coat, then she came up with the gun, and—"

"And what?" Mason asked.

"And shot him."

"Why?"

"Because he wouldn't give her brother a break and accept restitution."

"There wasn't to be any restitution," Mason said. "The brother had gone back and cleaned out the whole deal. Right then, they had the trump card. They had probably fifteen to twenty thousand dollars of Fremont's money. If Fremont sent Rodney to prison, Fremont was never going to see a dime of that money. No, Paul, that theory may be the one the district attorney has, and I hope it is, because I can poke some holes in it, in front of a jury."

"You can't poke enough holes in it to keep it from holding water," Drake said. "And remember, Perry, this is one case you can't win by cross-examining the prosecution's witnesses. The evidence in this case is cold, hard and mathematical.

"Probably tomorrow afternoon the prosecution is going to dump the whole thing in your lap, and then you've got to turn around and say, 'Nancy Banks, take the stand please,' and she's got to go on the stand and tell a story that's a convincing story. And, believe me, it's got to be a damned sight better than anything she's told you to date."

"What makes you say that?" Mason asked.

"The expression on your face, for one thing," Drake said.

Mason got up and began pacing the floor. "The deuce of it is," he said, "this is a case where Nancy would have been better off with another lawyer. It's a case that I shouldn't be handling."

"Why not?" Drake asked.

"Because," Mason said, "I believe in the truth. I like to get at the facts. That's all right when you have a client who's innocent, but when you have a client who has committed a crime, even if there are a lot of extenuating circumstances, the situation is different.

"Many criminal attorneys don't let their clients tell them a story. They wait until they see what the prosecution's evidence is, then they find the holes in that evidence and *then* have their client get on the stand and tell a story that fits in with the facts and takes enough advantage of the weak spots in the prosecution's case to be plausible, and it embarrasses the hell out of the prosecution.

"Of course, those attorneys don't tell their clients to get on the stand and commit perjury, but they *do* point out that *if* the client's story happens to be so-and-so and such-and-such, the jury would be apt to believe it. The client is smart enough to put two and two together and do the rest. That's why those attorneys never let their clients tell them their story in the first place, because if they don't know what the story is, there's nothing for the client to change and the attorney isn't guilty of suborning perjury."

"She couldn't tell a story in this case that would help any," Drake said.

"I don't know," Mason said. "She's a pretty clean-cut young woman. She makes quite an impression."

"I know, I know," Drake said. "That used to work before they put women on juries. You'd get a girl with good-looking legs and she literally could get by with murder. Now they have women on juries, and women look them over pretty damned carefully. If they show too much leg, it means they've alienated the votes of every woman on the jury. If they don't show leg, the men aren't influenced."

"She wouldn't have to show leg," Mason said. "She could simply tell a story which *may* be pretty close to what happened."

"Such as what?"

"She went to the motel; she was to meet her brother there."

"Do you think that's why she went there?"

"I'm satisfied it is. That's the logical explanation. She went out to this motel and had me put up bail for her brother. She felt that they would make an attempt to shadow her brother, also try to claim her winnings the same way they had Rodney's. She wanted to have a chance to talk with Rodney and find out exactly what he'd been doing, how much he'd embezzled and what the situation was."

Drake snapped his fingers. "Sure," he said, "that's the explanation of the whole business. The brother came out there. The brother was there. Fremont came out. They had an argument. The brother told him, 'Send me to jail and you'll never see a dime of your twenty thousand dollars or whatever the amount was. Moreover, I'll blab what I know to the income tax boys, and they'll have you on the carpet inside of twenty-four hours.' "

"And then?" Mason asked.

"Then Fremont made a pass at him, young Banks drove a fist into his stomach, knocked him back into the shower bath and . . . "

"Then what?" Mason asked.

"Well," Drake said lamely, "then Fremont drew his gun and Banks took it away from him and killed him."

"How did Banks take the gun away from him?" Mason asked. "You've left Fremont sitting in the shower, pointing a gun at Banks. Now, how did Banks move in on Fremont and take the gun away from him without getting shot?"

"The girl must have made some play at about that time,"

Drake said. "She must have made a grab for the gun or distracted Fremont's attention in some way."

"All right," Mason said, "keep talking."

Drake started to say something, then checked himself. "Hell, Perry, I'd have to have enough time to think up a story. . . . You could cross-examine me right now and . . . "

Mason suddenly snapped his fingers.

"What gives?" Drake asked. "You got something?"

Mason said, "I've just figured out why Hamilton Burger is in the case personally."

"Why?"

"Remember, he made some statements to the effect that the case was going to involve a matter which required the presence of the duly elected officer in charge of the prosecution, or something of that sort?"

Della Street nodded. "I took surreptitious notes of that," she said.

"Just what did he say?" Mason asked.

Della Street opened her notebook, turned the pages, came to the part and read:

> "Yes, Your Honor. I will be assisted by my trial deputy, Robert Calvert Norris, who is here in court with me. But, for the most part, I intend to handle the case myself. . . . As a matter of fact, for reasons which will appear as the case develops, this is going to be a very important case and a unique case and one in which it will be necessary for the duly elected district attorney of this county to take a personal part. There are legal issues involved which will probably establish a precedent in this county. . . . "

"That clinches it," Mason said. "He's there to grant immunity."

"What do you mean?"

147

"He's going to call Rodney Banks as a witness."

"Good heavens! You mean Banks will testify against his sister?"

"He won't have any choice in the matter," Mason said. "Burger is going to question him about the embezzlement, and Rodney is going to state that he refuses to answer questions on the advice of counsel, that the answers would tend to incriminate him and that he has been advised by counsel that such is the case.

"Thereupon, Burger is going to stand up and file an application with the Court to have the Court order him to answer the question anyway, and state that as far as the particular crime is concerned that Rodney is going to testify to, the prosecution will grant him full immunity."

"Then Rodney will have to answer the question?" Della Street asked.

Mason nodded. "It's a relatively new law."

"And that would put you in a position of—"

"Being right smack behind the eight ball," Mason said. "Paul, go in the other room. Get on the phone. You have an operative who's keeping track of Rodney Banks?"

Drake nodded.

"Relay the word to that operative to make a contact, in a friendly sort of way, or else get some damned good-looking woman operative, get her in a position where she can strike up an acquaintance with Rodney and tell him, as a tip, that the D.A. is going to put him on the stand, force him to answer questions by giving him immunity."

"What good will that do? It will simply make him leave the country, won't it?"

Mason smiled. "It will at least let him be prepared so that they won't catch us flat-footed by surprise."

"Rodney has been in touch with an attorney," Paul Drake said. "A fellow by the name of Jarvis N. Gilmore."

"Jarvis, huh?" Mason said, and smiled thoughtfully.

"You know him?" Drake asked.

"I know of him, and I know how he works," Mason said.

"For your information, the 'N' stands for a very unusual middle name—Nettle—and Jarvis is the boy who can nettle the district attorneys. I understand that while they hate me, they have a certain respect for me because I insist on truth. But Jarvis is a little the other way. They hate his guts and they lose just about all the cases Jarvis defends."

"You mean he doesn't insist on truth?"

"Confidentially," Mason said, "I was thinking of Jarvis Gilmore when I mentioned the type of attorney who listens to all of the evidence on behalf of the prosecution, then asks for a recess in order to prepare his defense, then gives the defendant a thorough coaching as to what his story should be, in order to take advantage of every possible weak point in the prosecution's case.

"After he's done that, he stalls for time just as much as possible, so that if there's any chance he gets an evening adjournment before he has to put his client on the stand. By that time the client has been coached, cross-examined and recross-examined and can tell a fairly convincing, straight-forward story and make it stand up under cross-examination."

"Well, Rodney Banks has consulted Gilmore."

Mason said, "So that accounts for the fact Gilmore just sort of looked in on the case a couple of times this afternoon. I'll tell you what you do, Paul. We can beat this all to pieces. Go to a phone booth where the call can't possibly be traced. Ring up Jarvis Gilmore."

"At this hour?" Drake asked.

"Hell, at any hour," Mason said. "My night telephone is unlisted. You'll find that Jarvis Gilmore is different. He has a day number and a night number, and, what's more, he has somebody who will answer the phone at any hour of the day or night. He's glad to get calls."

"Okay. What do I do?"

"Disguise your voice, tell him that you're a friend, that the district attorney is going to put his client on the stand

and force him to answer questions by giving him immunity."

"And then what?" Drake asked.

"Then hang up and get out of there and forget you ever put the call through," Mason said, grinning. "This just *may* give our friend, the district attorney, something to think about."

"You mean Jarvis Gilmore is that good?" Drake asked.

"I mean Jarvis Gilmore is that bad," Mason said. "Go ahead and get started, Paul."

Chapter 16

Judge Miles ascended to the bench and seated himself.

The bailiff said, "Everybody sit down, please."

Judge Miles observed, "The defendant is in court and the jurors are all present, gentlemen. Are you ready to proceed with the case?"

"Yes, Your Honor," Hamilton Burger replied.

"Yes, Your Honor, we are quite ready," Mason announced.

Norris rose to his feet. "Call Larsen E. Halstead to the stand."

Halstead's name was shouted down the corridor, and after a few moments he appeared in the courtroom, went to the witness stand and was sworn.

"You were, for some months prior to the time of Marvin Fremont's death, employed by him?"

"I was."

"Are you acquainted with Rodney Banks, the brother of the defendant?"

"I am."

"Where did you know him?"

"He also was employed by Marvin Fremont."

"What were your duties?"

"Well," Halstead said, looking over his glasses at the jury. "I was sort of a bookkeeper, office manager, income tax man and, I guess, general roustabout."

"And what did Rodney Banks do?"

"Well, he was a collector, a salesman and sort of a general utility man. Fremont's business was unconventional and people just didn't fit into regular patterns in that business, because the business didn't fit into a regular pattern."

"I see," Norris said. "Now, how much of that business was done on a cash basis?"

Halstead pursed his lips thoughtfully. "A great deal more than I suspected," he said, at length.

"Now, that answer is rather indefinite," Norris said, turning to the jurors to make certain they received the implication. "I'll go at it this way. Did the decedent keep large sums of cash in his office?"

"Very large sums."

"Which you knew about?"

"Some that I knew about and some I didn't find out about until later."

"Were the books carried in such a way that these sums of money were reflected in the books?"

"No, sir. These sums of money were different. They were kept in the form of cash, and it was, so to speak, an unregistered cash. No one knew it was there—no one except Fremont."

"Where was it kept?"

"There were two places. One of them was the safe, and the other one was a secret receptacle underneath the rug, under a cement block that could be lifted out."

"I show you photographs of the floor of the office. I am asking you if you can designate which one of the sections in this floor is the piece of cement you have reference to."

"This one."

"Now I show you a photograph of a section of cement lifted from the floor and ask you whether that is, or is not, the section of cement you have been describing."

"It is."

"And what is underneath this section of cement?"

"A metal box fixed in cement, immovable."

"And what was in this box the last time you saw it?"

"Nothing."

"I mean, the time before the last time you saw it."

"There was eighteen thousand, six hundred and ninety dollars in there."

"You counted this?"

"I counted it."

"Why?"

"Because I was making out the income tax returns and I certainly didn't intend to be a party to making out any false returns. As soon as I found out his cash was there, I decided to ask Mr. Fremont about it and see what he had to say, see what his explanation was, and then ask him to show me where this cash asset had been reflected in his books."

"Did you do that?"

"No, sir."

"Why not?"

"Mr. Fremont was murdered before I had an opportunity to put the matter up to him."

"Now, when was the time that you counted the money and found something over eighteen thousand dollars there?"

"That was Friday, a little before noon."

"Did you keep any records of what you found beyond the total amount?"

"Yes, I thought that I would try to check the turnover on some of the bills. For the most part, the bills were in ten- and twenty-dollar denominations, with quite a few fives and here and there a fifty. But there were several hundred-dollar bills in there, and I wrote down the numbers of four of those hundred-dollar bills."

"Do you have those numbers with you?"

"I do."

"Will you produce them, please, and by using that memo to refresh your recollection, tell the jurors what those numbers were?"

"Yes, sir."

"Will you please read those numbers to the jury. Tell the jury what the numbers were on those four one-hundred dollar bills."

"The numbers are L04824084A, L01324510A, G06300382A, and K00460975A."

"When did you write these numbers down?" Norris asked.

"At the time I counted the money."

"And what day was that?"

"That was on the second."

"On Friday, the second."

"That's right, yes."

"At what time did you say?"

"Shortly before noon. About eleven-thirty-five, I would say, as nearly as I can fix the time. I didn't make a note of the exact time, but it was at about eleven-thirty-five. Mr. Fremont went out at eleven-thirty, and I thought I would make a check."

"Do you know where he went?"

"He said he wouldn't be back any more that afternoon. I don't know where he went, no."

"Cross-examine," Norris said.

"I may not have any questions," Mason said, "but I would certainly like to inspect the memorandum which the witness used in refreshing his recollection."

"No objection whatever," Norris said.

Mason stepped forward and the witness handed Mason a small notebook, in which entries had been kept with the meticulously neat hand of a professional accountant. The numbers of the hundred-dollar bills concerning which he had testified were written so clearly that there could be no question of any mistake.

Mason gravely inspected the memo, then handed the notebook back to the witness.

"No questions," Mason said casually.

Norris said, with something of a gesture, "If the Court please, we wish to call Officer Moulton back to the stand."

"Very well," Judge Miles said. "Mr. Moulton to the stand."

The officer returned.

"You've already been sworn and you're still under oath," Judge Miles cautioned. "Take the stand."

Norris approached the witness, whipped a hundred-dollar bill from his pocket and said, "Mr. Moulton, I hand you a hundred-dollar bill. I call your attention to the number, which is K00460975A, and I am asking you if you have ever seen that hundred-dollar bill before. Please compare the number carefully before you answer the question."

Moulton took a notebook from his pocket, held the notebook and the bill together on his knee, then straightened and said, "Yes, I have seen that before."

"Where did you see it?"

"I recovered it from Rodney Banks."

"Is Rodney Banks, to your knowledge, related to the defendant in this case?"

"He is her brother."

"Now, you recovered this bill from him?"

"Yes."

"Did he make any statement as to where the bill came from?"

"Now, just a moment," Mason said. "That is objected to as calling for hearsay evidence."

"The objection is sustained."

"It is preliminary only, if the Court please," Norris said. "I will stipulate that the question may be answered yes or no."

"Under those circumstances, the Court's ruling will be that the question may be answered yes or no. Now understand, Mr. Moulton, the question is simply: Did he make a statement to you as to where he had received the bill, and you can answer that question yes or no."

"Yes," Moulton said.

"Later on, after that statement had been made, did you talk with the defendant, Nancy Banks?"

"I did."

"Did you make a statement in her presence?"

"I did."

155

"And what was that statement?"

"Now, just a moment," Mason said. "That is objected to as not being proper evidence, incompetent, irrelevant and immaterial. It makes no difference what the officer may have said to Nancy Banks."

"I understand that, Your Honor," Norris said, "but I want to connect this up. I want to have it appear that he made a statement to her, and her answer to that statement is what I want to get in evidence."

"I will go so far as to let him testify as to the statement," Judge Miles said, "although I will do so only on the assurance of the prosecutor that an answer was made by her which he considers pertinent."

"I so assure the Court."

"The objection is overruled. Answer the question."

Moulton said, "I told her that her brother said this hundred-dollar bill was part of some money that she had given him."

"And what did she say in relation to that statement?" Norris asked.

"Objected to as incompetent, irrelevant and immaterial," Mason said.

"Overruled."

"She said that she had nothing to say, that her attorney, Perry Mason, was going to make all statements for her."

"Now, just a minute," Judge Miles said. "I am not presently familiar with the rulings on a situation of this sort, but that doesn't seem to be an admission against interest."

"It's a part of the fact for the jurors to consider."

Judge Miles said, "I let this evidence in on the strength of an assurance by the prosecution that there was an answer that was pertinent. I had assumed that the answer would have been an admission on the part of the defendant that such had been the case; but this is certainly a far cry from that. The defendant certainly has a right not to talk with officers and not to answer their questions if she so chooses. . . . On thinking the matter over, I am going to reserve my ruling, I'm going to strike out these answers, I'm going to advise the jurors to disregard them.

"I will state to the jurors that, under the law, if an accusation is made to a defendant, and the defendant admits the accusation or makes some statement that indicates the accusation is true, the law permits that statement, the admission and the conduct of the defendant to be received in evidence. But in a case of this sort, I don't think the evidence comes within that rule. At least, as far as I'm concerned, it doesn't. I feel that a defendant at any time has a right to say, in effect, 'See my lawyer. He is making all statements for me.'

"You, ladies and gentlemen of the jury, will therefore disregard the evidence in regard to this statement made by the witness to the defendant, and her answer. That will be removed from your minds as evidence in the case."

"Under those circumstances," Hamilton Burger said, getting to his feet, his manner indicating that this was a situation which had been anticipated, "we will ask Officer Moulton to step down and I will call as a witness Lorraine Lawton."

When Lorraine had taken the stand, Norris said, "Your name is Lorraine Lawton, you live in an apartment directly across the hall from the defendant. You were present when Officer Moulton questioned Rodney Banks about where he had received the money that he had on his person?"

"Yes."

"You heard what Rodney Banks said?"

"Yes."

"Where did he say he had received all the money in his wallet? Who did he say had given it to him earlier in the evening?"

"Objection," Mason said. "Incompetent, irrelevant and immaterial, calling for hearsay evidence."

"Sustained," Judge Miles snapped.

"That's all," Norris said.

"No cross-examination," Mason said.

Lorraine Lawton left the stand.

"Call Rodney Banks," Burger said.

"You're calling Rodney Banks as your witness?" Judge Miles asked.

"Yes, Your Honor."

"Rodney Banks to the stand," the bailiff called.

Rodney Banks entered the courtroom accompanied by an undersized, very dapper individual, who came bustling forward ahead of the witness and said, "If the Court please, I am Jarvis Nettle Gilmore. I wish to have the record show that I am appearing as counsel for Rodney Banks at this point."

"Very well, Mr. Gilmore," Judge Miles said. "The record will so show."

"Hold up your right hand and be sworn," Gilmore instructed his client.

Rodney marched forward, held up his right hand, was sworn, took the witness stand, gave his name, address and turned to the district attorney with an expression of sullen defiance.

Hamilton Burger said, "I will examine this witness, if the Court please."

He turned to Rodney Banks. "Do you remember the occasion when you were arrested for embezzlement?"

"I do."

"And released on bail?"

"Yes."

"On the day that you were released, did you or did you not receive some money from your sister, the defendant in this case?"

"Objected to as incompetent, irrelevant and immaterial," Mason said. "Furthermore, the question is leading and suggestive and calls for a matter outside the scope of this case entirely."

"We intend to connect the matter up," Hamilton Burger said. "As far as the witness is concerned, he is plainly hostile and I have a right to ask leading questions."

"The Court will permit an answer to that question, but it can be answered yes or no," Judge Miles said.

"Did you receive money from your sister on that occasion?" Hamilton Burger thundered.

"Yes."

"Now then, I show you a hundred-dollar bill numbered K00460975A and ask you if that was part of the money that was given you by your sister."

"I refuse to answer on the ground the answer may incriminate me."

"Subsequently on that day, you met Officer Stanley Moulton?"

"Well, I think it was later on. I think that was a little after midnight. I think it was on Sunday morning, the fourth, that I met Moulton."

"But on that occasion, Moulton had a search warrant for your apartment, did he not?"

"He did."

"And he searched your apartment?"

"He did."

"And from your possession he took a hundred-dollar bill?"

"Yes."

"Now then," Hamilton Burger said, "where did you get that hundred-dollar bill?"

"Just a minute, just a minute, just a minute," Jarvis Gilmore intoned, striding forward and interposing his dapper body between the district attorney and the witness. "I advise you not to answer that question on the ground that the answer may tend to incriminate you."

"On the advice of counsel," Rodney Banks said, "I refuse to answer the question on the ground that to do so would incriminate me."

Judge Miles said, "Just a minute, I'll ask the questions here for a moment. Mr. Banks, have you disclosed what your answer to this question would have been to your counsel, Mr. Gilmore?"

"Yes, sir."

"Have you made a full, fair, frank disclosure to him of the circumstances?"

"Yes, sir."

"And you have been advised by Mr. Gilmore that if you answered that question you would incriminate yourself?"

"Yes, sir."

Judge Miles turned to Gilmore. "You have advised your client not to answer this question on the ground that the answer would incriminate him, and you are fully familiar with the facts in the case?"

"Yes, Your Honor."

"Under the circumstances," Judge Miles said, "the witness cannot be compelled to answer the question."

"Now, just a moment," Hamilton Burger said. "There is, if the Court please, a relatively new procedure and I am prepared to go forward under that procedure.

"I am fully familiar with the facts in this case. I have here a written request to Your Honor to order the witness to answer the question, notwithstanding the fact that it may, technically, incriminate him. I have prepared a written statement in which I grant this witness immunity from any crime in which he may technically have participated in connection with accepting this money.

"I ask the Court to have a hearing in this matter forthwith and instruct the witness that he has been granted immunity from prosecution and order him to answer the question."

"Let me see that written statement," Judge Miles said. "And I presume you have a copy for Perry Mason, as attorney for the defense, and for the witness?"

"And for the witness' attorney," Hamilton Burger said, proceeding to hand the judge the paper, then presenting copies, with something of a flourish, to Gilmore, to Perry Mason and to Rodney Banks.

Judge Miles read the document carefully. "This document, by its terms, Mr. Gilmore, provides that your client, Rodney Banks, is to be granted immunity and is hereby granted immunity from any technical violation of the law or any crime which may have resulted from his receiving stolen property from his sister."

"That isn't sufficient," Gilmore said. "The district attorney has asked a question. The district attorney can't force this witness to answer that question, unless he specifically states that the witness is given complete immunity from any crime which may be disclosed by answering that question."

"If counsel will keep on reading," Hamilton Burger said, "he will note that in the following paragraph the point he raises is covered. This is a standard form which I have used. I inserted the specific paragraph counsel is now complaining about, because I wanted to anticipate an objection that the form was too general. But you will notice in the printed form, it is stated that immunity is hereby granted to any crime disclosed by answering the question to which the witness refused an answer on the ground that to answer would incriminate him."

Judge Miles said, "Very well. I will conduct a hearing. I think perhaps that that is the spirit of the law, and I should follow the letter of the law.

"Mr. Banks, you have stated that to answer this question you would involve yourself in a crime, technically or otherwise."

"Yes, sir."

"And that your attorney has so advised you?"

"Yes, sir."

"And that you are refusing to answer this question solely on the ground that to do so would incriminate you?"

"Yes, sir."

"Within the limits of this county?"

"Yes, sir."

"It now appears, Mr. Banks, that Mr. Hamilton Burger, who is, and the Court will assure you he is, the duly elected, qualified and acting district attorney of this county, has, under the provision of the law and the powers vested in him by law, granted you complete immunity from prosecution for any crime which may be disclosed as a result of answering the question.

"Now then, under those circumstances, the Court assures you that immunity has been granted you and, therefore, under the provisions of the law, you no longer have the protection of the provisions against self-incrimination. I therefore instruct you that you have been granted complete immunity for the crime and that it is now your duty to answer the question."

Banks said, "Yes, sir."

"Do you understand the situation?" Judge Miles asked.

"Yes, sir."

"Very well. The question was where you received the hundred-dollar bill which Officer Moulton took from your possession."

"I think, if the Court please," Perry Mason said, "the Court should not paraphrase the question. I think that the court reporter should read the question to the witness."

"Very well, the court reporter will read the question," Judge Miles said, somewhat irritably. "I think you will find the Court's statement of the question was essentially fair. I just want to be sure that the witness understands his position and the fact that he has been granted immunity.

"I think both Court and counsel understand the situation fully. There have been instances in the past where a constitutional guarantee against self-incrimination has been distorted beyond the contemplation of the framers of the Constitution. People who don't want to answer questions have retained counsel, who have advised them that there may be a technical crime involved and therefore they are within their rights in refusing to answer on the ground that the answer would incriminate them.

"The law has now stepped in and has given the district attorney of the county the power to grant immunity to witnesses for such crimes, and this technical defense, or loophole of escape is no longer open to an unwilling witness."

Judge Miles frowned at Perry Mason as much as to intimate that the lawyer would receive better treatment at the hands of the Court if he refrained from questioning the Court's course of conduct.

"Yes, Your Honor," Mason said, with due humility.

"The court reporter will now read the question," Judge Miles said.

The court reporter read the question: "Now then, where did you get that hundred-dollar bill?"

"You understand that question?" Judge Miles asked the witness.

"Yes, sir."

"Answer it, then."

Rodney Banks looked at Gilmore. "Do I have to?"

"You have to. The Court has so directed. You have been granted immunity from any crime which will be disclosed as a result of your answer."

The witness said, "I got that hundred-dollar bill from the body of Marvin Fremont after I murdered him"

"What!" Hamilton Burger shouted, jumping to his feet.

Rodney Banks said nothing

Jarvis Gilmore smiled, a smirking smile, and made a little bow in the direction of the irate district attorney.

"I would like to have the court reporter read that answer," Perry Mason said. "Not only do I want to make certain it is in the record, but I want to make certain that I understand it and that the jurors understand it."

"Just a minute!" Hamilton Burger shouted. "I want that answer stricken from the record. That isn't the answer that— Why, that isn't the correct answer. . . . This witness got this money from his sister, and he is now perjuring himself in order to give his sister a means of escape."

"If the Court please," Perry Mason said, "I assign that remark by the district attorney as prejudicial misconduct. The district attorney is testifying in this case and making

163

statements of fact which are not in evidence, in the presence of the jury."

"Exactly," Judge Miles said irritably. "The jurors will disregard the statement as to any evidenciary matter by the district attorney. The assignment of misconduct is allowed. The jurors are admonished to pay no attention to this.

"Now then, gentlemen, what's this all about?"

"First, if the Court please," Mason said, "I want to have the court reporter read the answer of the witness to make certain that it's in the record and to make certain that I understand it."

"I object to having it read," Hamilton Burger said. "It is— Why, this is a matter which calls for disciplinary action by the Grievance Committee of the Bar Association. These attorneys, apparently anticipating what I had in mind, have rigged the cards in such a manner— Why, this is preposterous!"

"Do I understand," Mason asked, "that the district attorney is now objecting to having the court reporter read a part of the recorded proceedings?"

"I move to strike out the answer of the witness," Hamilton Burger said. "I want it stricken before it is read."

Judge Miles said, "This is a most extraordinary situation. I can understand that the district attorney is taken by surprise, but, as was pointed out in the preliminary discussion, this granting of immunity is on a printed form and there certainly is a statement here in the printed form that the witness is given immunity from *any* crime which may be disclosed in answering the question and in which the witness may have participated technically or *otherwise*."

"If the Court please," Mason asked, "may I renew my motion to have the court reporter read the question and answer?"

Judge Miles frowned at Mason, regarded the smirking countenance of Jarvis Gilmore, said irritably to the court reporter, "Read the answer to the question—read both question and answer."

164

The court reporter read the question, "Now then, where did you get that hundred-dollar bill?"

Then the court reporter turned the pages of his notebook and read: "The answer was, 'I got that hundred-dollar bill from the body of Marvin Fremont after I murdered him.'"

"Now then," Mason said, "we have again a question of the district attorney repeating his misconduct and making statements to the jurors of facts which are not in evidence."

"That is repeated misconduct," Judge Miles said. "I caution the district attorney that this is an unusual procedure, but the district attorney should keep his temper and his presence of mind. I again admonish the jurors not to pay any attention to any statements made by the prosecutor as to the facts in the case, unless those statements are supported by evidence.

"Do you wish to move for a mistrial, Mr. Mason, on account of the situation which has developed?"

Mason suppressed a smile. "No, Your Honor, I merely wish to have the Court caution the district attorney not to make statements as to evidenciary matters which are not supported by testimony, and to admonish the jurors to disregard those statements which have already been made."

Judge Miles gave the matter thoughtful consideration.

"Perhaps there should be a mistrial, under all the circumstances," Hamilton Burger said hopefully.

"I think the defendant has been placed on trial before a jury of her peers and is entitled to a verdict of acquittal at the hands of this jury," Mason said.

"I am going to prosecute this witness for perjury," Hamilton Burger blustered.

"And here again, if the Court please," Mason said, "we have an instance of misconduct—the district attorney, using his official position to intimidate a witness and discredit testimony which has been given in court."

Judge Miles permitted himself a smile. "I don't think the witness is intimidated," he said. "However, the district attorney will again be cautioned to remember that this is a criminal proceeding, that a jury is present and that this situation, while somewhat unprecedented, no doubt, is nevertheless the result of an action taken by the prosecutor.

"The record now shows that the witness was given immunity, that the witness answered the question, that the answer to the question disclosed a crime. Now, Mr. Prosecutor, do you have any more questions of this witness?"

"I certainly do," Hamilton Burger shouted.

"I think," Judge Miles said, "it would be better for the court to take a fifteen-minute recess at this time, and permit counsel for both sides to regain their emotional equilibrium and adjust themselves to these new developments in the case. The court will take a recess for fifteen minutes, and the jurors are admonished not to discuss the case among themselves or permit anyone else to discuss it in their presence."

Judge Miles had hardly left the bench before an irate Hamilton Burger came storming to the defense side of the courtroom.

"You can't get away with this!" he shouted at Gilmore. "I'm going to have you before the grand jury, not before the Grievance Committee of the Bar Association, mind you, but before the grand jury.

"I'm going to have you indicted for conspiracy to commit perjury and as an accessory after the fact in a murder case. You know just as well as I do that this young man got the money from his sister, and you jockeyed me into a position where I granted him immunity to the answer to the question and then fixed it so the answer to the question threw me for a loss in this case."

"Go ahead, get me before the grand jury," Gilmore said. "Prosecute Rodney for perjury. In order to prove any perjury, you'll first have to prove he did *not* kill Fremont. That'll be a great trial scene, the district attorney of the county trying to prove a man innocent of murder and the man insisting he's guilty. I'm really looking forward to *that* show."

"Is that true? Would you have to prove he *didn't* commit the murder?" one of the newspaper reporters asked Burger.

Hamilton Burger whirled on him, and as he whirled, the action was frozen with a flashbulb.

A gleeful newspaper reporter scurried from the courtroom with a picture of a district attorney who had completely lost control of his emotions.

"Take it easy, Hamilton," Mason said. "You're not getting anywhere with this sort of a display."

Burger took a deep breath, said, "I hadn't anticipated any such tactics on *your* part."

"Not on *my* part," Mason said. "This isn't doing you any good. You've walked into a trap—now then, do you want to stay in it or do you want to get out of it and go on with the case? I may be able to help you."

"There isn't any case to go on with," Burger said.

Mason moved closer to him, hooked his arm in that of the irate district attorney's, said, "If you keep on talking like this, there won't be any career for *you* to go on with. Take this thing in your stride. Now, come down to earth."

Burger said, "I hate to be trapped by such a despicable little shyster. We all know Gilmore. The guy doesn't hesitate any more at suborning perjury than you do in crossing the street."

"Take it easy, take it easy," Mason said. "Now, go get yourself a drink of water, start smiling and let's go on with the case."

"What case?" Burger asked. "It's all done now—all except the shouting."

"And you're doing the shouting," Mason told him. "Cool off and let me cross-examine Rodney Banks. Don't let the public feel that Gilmore outwitted you."

"I knew he was crooked," Burger said, "but I didn't know he'd go to such lengths as all this."

"You don't *know* that he coached Rodney on this,"

Mason said. "Calm down, take it easy. I don't like to see you—"

Burger took a deep breath. "All right," he said, "only dammit, I feel that you've had a finger in this pie somewhere."

"I did," Mason told him, smiling, "but I didn't have my thumb in it. It was the thumb that pulled out the plum, if you'll remember your nursery rhyme."

Burger glared at him, stalked away, brushed aside newspaper reporters with a terse "No comment" and walked over to confer with Lt. Tragg.

In the meantime, word having been flashed over the wires of the startling developments in the case, the courtroom began to fill up with courthouse attachés, with more newspaper reporters and photographers with cameras and flash guns.

At the end of approximately twenty minutes, Judge Miles took the bench.

"Now, I note that there are several gentlemen of the press here," he said. "There are to be no photographs taken in court, no photographs in the courtroom during the presence of the jury, the defendant or of myself. Photographs can be taken in the corridor. Photographs can be taken in the courtroom after adjournment and after the jurors have left their places in the jury box.

"Now then, Mr. District Attorney, proceed with the case."

"I have no further questions of this witness," Hamilton Burger said. "I submit, if the Court please, that the answer given to the question was obviously for the purpose of benefiting his sister, the defendant in this case, rather than for the purpose of clarifying the issues, and I ask that the Court order this man into custody."

"The Court has no authority to order him into custody at this time, nor does the Court care to pass upon the issues. The jurors will receive the evidence, and when the case is finally submitted to them, render a verdict.

"Now, then, Mr. Banks, you have testified and you have been excused."

"I've been granted immunity for the murder?" Banks asked.

"The Court doesn't care to comment on the legal aspect of the situation as far as you are concerned," Judge Miles said, with obvious distaste. "You have an attorney who is representing you—an attorney," the judge added, with a certain amount of grudging admiration, "who seems to be fully capable of giving you completely adequate representation.

"You may leave the stand, Mr. Banks."

"Just a minute," Mason said. "I have the right to cross-examine the witness."

Judge Miles hesitated for a moment, then said thoughtfully, "Yes, you have that *right*."

"I have a few questions to ask on cross-examination," Mason said.

"Very well, you may proceed."

Perry Mason sized up the witness warily. "You had been betting money on the horse races from time to time?"

"Over the weekends, yes."

"And you had embezzled money from your employer in order to make good your losses?"

"Just a minute, Your Honor," Gilmore said. "That question is objected to as calling for the witness to incriminate himself and is asking for facts which are incompetent, irrelevant and immaterial and not connected with the present controversy, and I direct my client, the witness, not to answer the question on the ground that the answer will incriminate him."

"Do you feel that the answer to that question would incriminate you?" Judge Miles asked.

"Yes, Your Honor."

"And you have been advised by your attorney not to answer on the ground that the answer would incriminate you, and you do place your refusal to answer on that ground."

"Yes, Your Honor."

"Under the circumstances, in view of the way the question is phrased, the Court certainly feels that the Court cannot force the witness to answer that question unless the district attorney cares to grant complete immunity. Does the district attorney care to do so?"

"The district attorney does not care to do so," Hamilton Burger said. "The district attorney has already been thrown out on one of these squeeze plays by Mason to Gilmore to Banks. The district attorney not only doesn't intend to grant any further immunity to this witness, but the district attorney intends to prosecute this witness for any crime which has been committed within this jurisdiction and which was not included in the immunity granted earlier in the day."

Again partially losing control of himself, Hamilton Burger said, "I'll prosecute him for embezzlement, I'll prosecute him for speeding. I'll prosecute him for spitting on the sidewalk."

"Under the circumstances," Judge Miles said, smiling slightly, "there certainly is no ground on which the Court can instruct the witness to answer."

"Now then," Mason said, "when you knew that discovery was imminent, you went to the secret receptacle which you had found in the office and cleaned out all of the cash that was in there, did you not?"

"Don't answer, don't answer, don't answer," Gilmore said "The answer will incriminate you."

Gilmore turned to Judge Miles and said, "I must protest this form of cross-examination. Counsel very well knows what he is doing. He is putting my client in great jeopardy. The Court has heard the district attorney make his declaration—"

"There's no need to make a speech about it," Judge Miles said. "Make an objection."

"I object that the question calls for an answer which would incriminate my client, and I advise my client not to answer on the ground that the answer would incriminate him."

"You have heard the statement of your attorney," Judge Miles said to Rodney Banks. "Is that your position?"

"That's my position."

"Under the circumstances," Judge Miles said, "the position of the witness is well taken, that the answer would incriminate him, and the Court sees no reason to order him to answer."

"That concludes my cross-examination," Mason said.

"Oh, Your Honor," Hamilton Burger said, "this is hopeless. This is becoming a farce. The prosecution feels that—"

Mason got to his feet, said, "May I interpolate a remark to the Court?"

"What is it?" Judge Miles asked. "I think, Mr. Mason, your client's interest would best be served by letting the district attorney continue with what he is about to state. As I size up the situation, he is about to make a motion."

"Before he makes that motion," Mason said, "I would like to recall one witness for cross-examination."

"What witness?"

"Mrs. Lorraine Lawton."

Hamilton Burger started to object, then suddenly, with a crafty look in his eye, settled back in his chair.

"Is there any objection on the part of the district attorney?" Judge Miles asked.

"No objection," Burger said.

Judge Miles regarded Mason thoughtfully. "I wish to state, Counselor, that as far as your client is concerned, the case would seem to be in such a present situation that the cross-examination of a prosecution's witness would hardly improve her position, whereas there is always the possibility that it might be affected adversely."

"I understand that, if the Court please," Mason said.

"And may I state, on behalf of the defendant, that this defendant does not want to be acquitted on a technicality or under such circumstances that there will be a cloud on her name. The defendant would like to establish the truth, the real truth, the whole truth."

"Never mind the fireworks," Hamilton Burger said. "Skip the oratory. Go ahead, recall the witness, and be careful you don't put *your* foot into a trap."

"Counsel's remark," Judge Miles said, "is completely uncalled for. The Court can appreciate the trying circumstances with which the prosecution's office is confronted, but the Court does not intend to relax decorum because of that fact. Now, Mr. Mason, you wished to recall Mrs. Lorraine Lawton?"

"Yes, Your Honor."

"Mrs. Lorraine Lawton, back to the stand," Judge Miles ordered.

When Lorraine Lawton entered the courtroom, Judge Miles said, "There is no need for you to be sworn again. You have already been sworn. Remember that your testimony is under oath. Mr. Mason has recalled you for further cross-examination. Proceed, Mr. Mason."

Mason said, "You are friendly with the defendant?"

"Yes."

"And with her brother?"

"Yes."

"You work at a trout farm known as Osgood Trout Farm?"

"Yes."

"That's already been gone over," Hamilton Burger said.

"This is preliminary merely," Mason said, "in order to see that I do not take unfair advantage of the witness."

"Proceed," Judge Miles ruled.

"You saw Rodney Banks after he had been released on bail on the evening of the third?"

"Yes."

"You knew that Rodney Banks was leaving you in order

172

to keep an appointment with his sister at Unit 14 at the Foley Motel, a motel with which you are fully familiar and which is near the trout farm which you sometimes operate?"

"Yes."

"Did you go to the Osgood Trout Farm that evening?"

"I . . . I . . . I don't think I care to answer that question."

"Did you go to the Osgood Trout Farm and get some packages of dry ice?" Mason asked.

"I . . . "

"Now, just a minute," Mason said, holding up his hand. "Before you answer that question, I want to call your attention to certain facts. Rodney Banks has admitted to the murder of Marvin Fremont. He has been given immunity by the district attorney from prosecution. Now then, I understand that your conduct may be technically illegal, but I think the authorities will be interested in uncovering the truth and I think they will make concessions to you if you tell the absolute truth. . . . Now, didn't you go to the Osgood Trout Farm that evening?"

"I—I don't think I should answer that question. I think that would incriminate me."

"That depends," Mason said. "If you found the body of Marvin Fremont, if you thought that Rodney Banks had killed him, and if you felt that you could pack the body in dry ice long enough to lower the body temperature so that the police would feel the crime was committed at a time when Rodney was in jail and therefore had a perfect alibi, you have committed a crime. That, however, will always remain a matter between you and your own conscience. It is not going to affect Rodney's chances of conviction because he has been given immunity."

"That's not exactly what I did," she said. "I knew that Rodney was in a dangerous mood as far as Marvin Fremont was concerned. I knew that he knew that Marvin Fremont was going to call on Nancy, that he knew where she was, and I was afraid of what Rodney might do. . . . I had, of course, seen Rodney after his release from jail, but later on we pretended we hadn't seen each other.

"I went to the motel, the door was open. Nancy was not there, Rodney was not there. I went in to look around and found the body in the shower. Apparently he had been dead for only a short time. I was in a panic. Then I saw the body was packed in dry ice, and then I remembered Nancy's telling us about how body temperature determined the time of death, and I thought . . . well, I thought Rodney had killed him, that Nancy had gone to the farm, got some dry ice, packed the body in dry ice, and planned to leave it there for two or three hours, lower the temperature so the police would think the body had been dead for hours and hours, and thereby give Rodney an alibi because he had been in jail.

"So, of course, I didn't notify the police."

"Thank you," Mason said, "that's all "

Hamilton Burger got to his feet "Well, I feel that No questions on redirect."

"Now then," Mason said, "I would like to recall Larsen E. Halstead for one or two further questions."

"No objection," Hamilton Burger said, looking at Mason with thoughtful eyes in which there was a newfound respect.

"Recall Larsen Halstead," Judge Miles said. "And may I say, gentlemen, that I agree with Mr. Mason, that as far as the defendant is concerned, if we can get to the bottom of this thing it may not only clarify the situation but, in the long run, be in the best interests of justice. I submit that thought to the prosecution for consideration."

Larsen Halstead returned to the stand, adjusted his spectacles on his nose, glanced over them at Perry Mason.

"You state that when you last saw the secret receptacle it contained eighteen thousand, six hundred and ninety dollars?"

"That's right."

"And you took the numbers of four one-hundred dollar bills which were in there?"

"Yes."

"And that included the hundred-dollar bill which has now been introduced in evidence, number K00460975A?"

"Yes."

"And you state that Mr. Fremont had left the office for the day?"

"Yes. There is a chance, however, that it was he and not Rodney who returned later on in the day and removed the money. Perhaps it was the following morning, I don't know. All I know is that the money was there the last I saw of the place, but gone when I went there with the police."

"And, because you wanted to check on that money, you looked through a few of the larger bills in the pile and took down the numbers?"

"Yes."

"On a memo?"

"Yes."

. "And the number K00460975A appears on that list, together with the numbers of three other hundred-dollar bills?"

"Yes."

"May I see that list that you made, please," Mason said. "I want to check the numbers."

The witness wearily withdrew a wallet from his hip pocket, fumbled through it and took out a small notebook.

"Just a minute," Mason said. "You had that notebook in this compartment in the wallet?"

"Yes."

"May I see that compartment, please?"

The witness handed over the worn leather wallet.

Mason opened it, pulled out a hundred-dollar bill and said, "Now, the number on this hundred-dollar bill is L04824084A. And here's another hundred-dollar bill, G06309382A. There is a third hundred-dollar bill, number L0132—"

The witness grabbed at the wallet and the hundred-dollar bills Mason was holding in his hand.

Mason jerked the wallet back out of reach and said, "I will repeat: There is another hundred-dollar bill, number L01324510A.

"Now, then," Mason continued, "if you had nothing to do with the murder, if the bills were still in that receptacle when you left the office, how does it happen that these hundred-dollar bills are in *your* wallet?"

Halstead stared at Mason with panic-stricken eyes. "I guess I . . . I guess I must have been mistaken. I guess I must have put those hundred-dollar bills in my wallet instead of returning them to the vault. I was copying the numbers, and I must have inadvertently folded the hundred-dollar bills and put them in the wallet when I closed the notebook and put it in."

"Then," Mason said, "you must have also had the hundred-dollar bill which has been introduced in evidence, K00460975A."

"That's right, I guess I must have."

"Then," said, "how could that bill have been in the possession of Rodney Banks at the time of his examination by Officer Moulton unless you had surreptitiously inserted it in his wallet in the meantime?"

"I . . . I— There must have been some mistake in the number."

"No, Halstead," Mason said. "The mistake was on your part in thinking you could clean out the money in the vault and report to Fremont that Rodney Banks had taken the money. Then, when Fremont found out your perfidy and tried to force you at gunpoint to restore the money, you gave him a sudden push which sent him sprawling backwards into the shower and resulted in the gun going off and penetrating his heart. Or did you deliberately connive to get possession of the gun and then murder him?"

"No, no, I didn't. It was an accident—I refuse to answer

any more questions. There has been some mistake— I have been framed."

For a long moment it would have been possible to have heard the ticking of a clock. Then the courtroom broke into an uproar.

"Take that man into custody," Judge Miles ordered. "Court is going to take another fifteen-minute recess."

Chapter 17

Mason, Della Street, Paul Drake and Nancy Banks sat in the lawyer's office.

Nancy, half hysterical, said, "I still don't understand how you did it, Mr. Mason."

The lawyer grinned at Della Street and said, "I'm not sure that I do myself."

"Can you tell me what happened?" she asked. "So I can understand it."

Mason said, "Your brother hadn't found the secret store of cash which Fremont kept at the office, but he did know of the money in the safe, which at times ran into several hundred dollars.

"Fremont deliberately put temptation in your brother's way by having him make collections in cash on Friday afternoons after the banks had closed and having him keep the money until Monday morning. He knew that your brother went to the racetrack and did a lot of betting in a small way.

"Sooner or later the inevitable happened, and Rodney 'borrowed' some of Fremont's money to make a bet. After a while these borrowings became a habit, and then when Rodney hit a losing streak he was behind the eight ball. It was at this point that Fremont decided to spring the trap."

"But why?" she asked.

"Because," Mason said, "Fremont had always had his eye on you and had never forgiven you for slapping his face and walking out. He made up his mind he was going to make you come to him begging for mercy. He knew how fond of your brother you were and felt that once he had your brother arrested you'd be beseeching him to accept restitution and dismiss the complaint.

"Just as Fremont thought his plans were about to bear fruit, Rodney appealed to you, you made a bet on a long shot, and at the same time Rodney made a bet on a long shot.

"The horse came in to win, and Fremont was on hand to claim that the bet, having been made with embezzled money, was his property.

"He was furious that you had made a killing, that I had cashed the tickets and that he couldn't bluff me into surrendering the money.

"Fremont knew that I would pay the money over to you, less my fee, and knew that you would park your car in the parking lot at the apartment. He cut a mask out of a handkerchief and held you up, doubtless feeling that the money was his anyway and that it was no crime to take what belonged to him.

"After the holdup, however, he found the money was considerably less than the fourteen thousand he expected. He hadn't realized that we'd put up five thousand dollars bail for Rodney, or that you had given Rodney part of the winnings, but thought that you had concealed the bulk of the money.

"In some way, probably through his detective agency, he learned that you were staying at the Foley Motel, so he went down there to collect the rest of the money.

"What no one took into consideration was the fact that Halstead, knowing of the secret supply of money Fremont kept in the vault, felt that it would be a good time to clean out the whole supply of money and did so, knowing that the blame would fall on Rodney's shoulders.

"However, Fremont became suspicious of Halstead and accused him of stealing the money.

"Halstead followed Fremont to the Foley Motel.

"We only have Halstead's words as to what happened

there. But apparently his story is correct because the physical facts substantiate it.

"Halstead offered to make a deal with Fremont by which Halstead would be permitted to keep the money he had, the charge against Rodney would be dismissed, and Halstead in turn would say nothing to the authorities about Fremont receiving stolen property and being a high-class fence.

"Things didn't go as planned. The two men got in an argument. Fremont drew a gun. Halstead tried to rush the gun and grab it before Fremont could shoot. Fremont backed into the shower, his foot slipped, he fell and as he fell the gun was discharged.

"At that time the two men were struggling and the bullet penetrated Fremont's heart.

"Halstead was then in a panic. He had to cover up. Knowing that you had made this statement about dry ice and body temperature, knowing about the Osgood Trout Farm, he went out there. First he hid the gun in the trash barrel, then picked the lock, got a supply of dry ice and put it around Fremont's body. After that, he went to the place where he knew your brother had left a billfold containing a reserve supply of cash and planted one of the numbered hundred-dollar bills that he had been intending to use in case he had to frame Rodney and thereby give himself a clean bill of health."

"But how did you come to suspect Halstead had those other bills in his wallet?" Della Street asked.

"The answer," Mason explained, "was in the way the numbers on those hundred-dollar bills had been written down in the notebook.

"These were long numbers, yet each was carefully and neatly written, each on one line of the notebook.

"A man crouched on the floor couldn't have written those numbers that way. He would have to be seated at a desk with his arm resting on a level surface.

"Therefore it occurred to me that Halstead must have appropriated those hundred-dollar bills and written down the numbers so he could protect himself by planting some of the bills in Rodney's wallet, and, if he had a chance, planting some of the others where they would be found among Nancy's things.

"It was a long shot, but like the long shot on Dough Boy, it paid off."

Nancy impulsively threw her arms around the lawyer's neck.

"I'll say it paid off!"

Mason grinned. "And it's paying off now."

About the Author

Erle Stanley Gardner is the king of American mystery fiction. A criminal lawyer, he filled his mystery masterpieces with intricate, fascinating, ever-twisting plots. Challenging, clever, and full of surprises, these are whodunits in the best tradition. During his lifetime, Erle Stanley Gardner wrote 146 books, 85 of which feature Perry Mason.